"Harriet, my dearest, may I ask your papa for your hand?"

"Oh yes, but..." She paused. "Robert, I love you with all my heart, and I would be proud to be your wife. Only I am afraid Papa and Mama may not like it. You will not be hurt, will you?"

"I promise I shall not," he answered tenderly, knowing that when he revealed his true identity, they were likely to welcome him into the family with open arms. "But you..." he continued. "Will they not be angry with you?"

"Yes, I suppose they will. But I know they do truly desire my happiness, and when they see we are in earnest, they must agree in the end."

"And you would submit to all this for me?" he asked, much struck.

"Of course," said Harriet. "How can you doubt it?"

"Bravest of girls." He tightened his hold and kissed her again, feeling her body quiver in response to his eager kisses. After a few moments, she struggled from his hold.

"I must go back, Robert. Already Mama might be wondering where I am."

"Harriet! Wait! There is something I must tell you!"

But she was already among the trees. No matter. He would tell her in London. He could hardly wait to see her delight!

LADY HARRIET'S HARVEST

PETRA NASH

Harlequin Books

TORONTO • NEW YORK • LONDON
AMSTERDAM • PARIS • SYDNEY • HAMBURG
STOCKHOLM • ATHENS • TOKYO • MILAN

First published in Great Britain 1988
by Mills & Boon Limited.

Harlequin Regency Romance edition
published October 1990

ISBN 0-373-31136-2

Printed in U.S.A.

CHAPTER ONE

'So, YOU ARE come back. And not before time.' Lady Beatrice Fitzpaine looked down her aquiline nose at her great-nephew with eyes whose brightness belied her seventy years. Sir Robert thought, not for the first time, that she resembled nothing so much as an elderly, well-groomed eagle. For a moment his lips twitched with amusement as he crossed her elegant drawing room to kiss first her hand and then her proffered cheek. Then he felt the familiar sensation of unreality sweep over him. He blinked as the room blurred before his eyes, and attempted to speak normally.

'As you see, aunt. And very glad to see you in such good looks.'

'Fiddle-faddle,' responded his elderly relative. 'At my age I do not look for compliments on my looks. My teeth and my digestion are still sound, and I am thankful for that.'

If she felt his hand tremble in hers she gave no sign, but waved him to a seat in a peremptory fashion. He was glad to sit down, but cursed what he felt to be an unmanly weakness. For how long, he wondered, would the trivialities of daily conversation continue to summon up images of death, the spectres of cholera and typhoid that still haunted his dreams?

Lady Beatrice was silent as she watched his struggle for composure. Sir Robert Atherington looked, she thought, much older than his twenty-six years. The thin sunlight of January was unkind to him, lighting up the skin that had taken on a curiously yellow-grey tinge, shadowing the sunken eyes and fading some of the rich corn gold from his hair. Though it was nearly four months since he had been wounded in the taking of Sebastopol that had ended the war in the Crimea, he still looked a sick man. She sighed. The young man who had gone to war so vigorous, so full of pride in his new captaincy, had gone for ever, she feared. Even his once remarkable height seemed diminished, as though his large frame had somehow shrunk, withered away in the filth and degradation of Scutari.

He heard the sigh, and looked at her.

'You look dreadful,' she snapped.

'I know I do,' he replied ruefully. 'My clothes are quite out of fashion, and I even think I can detect a hint of moth-ball about them. I almost feared your butler would refuse me admittance.'

'Don't be ridiculous,' she replied without heat, realising that he was trying to cheer her. 'You know very well what I mean. Does your wound still pain you?'

'Not at all,' he lied. 'That is to say, not all the time,' he amended in answer to her sceptical look. 'I was lucky. The surgeon was able to extract the ball quite quickly, and my batman took good care of me.' A shadow crossed his face, and he fell silent.

'What you need,' said Lady Beatrice decidedly, 'is a wife.'

Sir Robert looked alarmed. 'A wife! My dear aunt, a wife is the last thing in the world that I need!'

'You are young, and well born, and your income is more than adequate to support a wife. Since you have now inherited the Hall you would pass, in the eyes of the world, as a wealthy man. It is your duty to marry.'

'The eyes of the world may see what they will. There is more to marriage than the possession of a sufficient income to support a family. In my own eyes I am not fit to be any woman's husband. I can hardly support to live with myself. How could I ask some sheltered female to live with me?' He rubbed a shaking hand across his face. 'I cannot forget, Aunt Beatrice. I can never forget.'

He stood up and paced to the window, looking with unseeing eyes at the elegant façade across the square. 'It is not the fighting, nor the dying. I went, as did many, prepared if necessary to give my life in a cause that seemed to me to be just. That I might die, that I might see my men die, I was prepared for. Soldiers must die, if they fight. But soldiers should die in battle, of their just wounds. Not of cold, and hunger, and filth.'

'It was so bad, then?'

'It was worse than you could believe.'

'I read Mr Russell's dispatches in *The Times*, of course, as everyone did. They caused a great deal of anger and dismay.'

'He did not tell the half of it. I have seen things, aunt, that haunt me yet. Things that are not fit to be spoken of in a lady's drawing room.'

'Miss Nightingale is a lady. Surely such things should be spoken of everywhere. How else can things be changed?'

'Most ladies would not agree with you. They would rather close their eyes to it all. The war has been won, what matter the cost?'

'I cannot agree with you. There may well be some who choose not to think, not to care, but there are many who do.'

'Among your acquaintance, perhaps. But the young girls I meet seem to have no thoughts above their dress, or the latest song, or the next ball.'

'That is hardly their fault, poor things. It is not proper for young girls to read newspapers. They can have no opinions on things of which they have no knowledge.'

'How, then, can they be considered fit partners for a man of sense?'

She looked at him with wry amusement. 'Few men choose a wife for companionship. For that they go to their club, their horse, or their dog. A wife may be chosen for her family connections, her wealth, her looks, or merely her suitability.'

'That will not do for me. I had no idea you were so cynical, aunt.'

'I am not saying that you should choose thus, I merely tell you how the world thinks. A wife may well become a companion and a friend, but that is usually something that happens after you are married, if you are lucky. It takes time, and shared experience, to build such a relationship. It is not possible during courtship, when you are unlikely ever to be alone with a girl for longer than a few minutes, and the most private conversations you are likely to have with her must be carried on as you dance. Do you number many married couples among your friends?'

'A few, of course, among acquaintances. But my friends . . . my friends are my brother officers, and few of them were in a position to be able to marry. It is not encouraged, you know, until a man has served for some years. Fortunately,' he added bitterly. 'This war has already left too many widows and fatherless children.'

He fell silent, gazing into the fire. Lady Beatrice waited without impatience. At length he drew breath, and turned to her with a rueful smile.

'The truth is, aunt, that I am in no state to be seeking a bride. The young women of my own class bore or irritate me, and yet I must marry a woman of breeding and education. I do not know what I want, but I fear she cannot exist.'

'Stuff and nonsense,' retorted Lady Beatrice without heat. 'You are as yet even less fit, in your bodily state, than you think you are. These blue devils are from lack of health and strength.'

'Shall I stay in Bath, then, and take the waters?'

'Certainly not. That is for old women like me. Fresh air, exercise, and good plain food are what I would prescribe. Why do you not spend some time on your new estate? I have heard it is badly in need of a master, and it is more than a year since Arthur Atherington died.'

'I have never seen it. You know Cousin Arthur would never accept that I was to be his heir.'

'He was a fool! His mother was just such a one, for ever complaining but never doing anything. Since he himself refused to marry and beget an heir, the entail must devolve on you. I knew him as a boy, when he stayed at Milborne Ducis while my grandmother was alive. A sullen boy, as I recall, who would never share his toys and always took the last piece of cake.'

Sir Robert gave an appreciative laugh. 'He does not seem to have improved with age! My lawyers tell me that for the last few years he lived almost as a recluse, with only two old servants to care for the Hall. He even grudged the money for a doctor for himself. By the time he was too weak to protest, it was too late for the doctor to help him.'

'His income was a good one, I believe?'

'Oh, yes, he simply wouldn't spend it. The ironical thing is that it has all come to me. How he would have hated that. His own economies meant that his income piled up, yet he could not make a will that would leave it away from me, as he might have done had he wished. The farm rents are down to nothing, of course. A bad master makes for bad tenants. I don't doubt there will be plenty for me to do, or that I shall need to dip deep into my pockets to set all to rights. Heigh-ho! Who'd be the heir to Atherington Hall?'

'Since your own pockets are far from to let, I waste no pity on you. Do you remain in Bath for any time?'

'No, I shall set out the day after tomorrow for London, to settle things with the lawyers, then go on to Atherington.'

'You'll not find much comfort there in January, by all accounts. What will you do about servants?'

'I shall take my batman. He is staying on with me as my manservant, and I can rely on him to see to my creature comforts. We have neither of us been used to soft living, and I have a fancy for a solitary life, for a while at least.'

The tight, bitter look had returned to his face. Lady Beatrice was not by nature a soft-hearted woman. Expecting no sympathy for herself she spent little on her fellow creatures, but she was fond of her great-nephew. It crossed her mind that while his bodily wounds might have healed more or less cleanly, this war in the Crimea had dealt more grievously with his spirit, and she mourned for the light-hearted boy he had been. As ever, she hid her gentler thoughts under a brusque exterior.

'Well, you have suffered, I make no doubt, and so did many. It is of little use to regret the past. You must look to the future, now, so that the suffering will not have been in vain.'

To her relief he raised one eyebrow over an eye that had regained its sparkle. 'You should have been in the Church, revered aunt! I am sure you would have been a bishop long since, if not an archbishop!'

She looked at him austerely.

'I am too old to be shocked by your irreverence. And you will see that I am right.' In her mind, though not aloud, she added, 'And what you need, my boy, is a good wife.'

For the rest of the afternoon she kept the conversation more impersonal. She was well able to bring him up to date with the doings of the Royal Family, and with the political happenings that had occurred during his absence, for though she lived retired she had a wide acquaintance, and was an indefatigable correspondent. By the time he went to dress for dinner he seemed more relaxed, and under the influence of a good meal and several glasses of excellent claret a sparkle came back to his face that she had missed, and it seemed to her that the striking good looks she had remembered were not altogether gone. While he might no longer be thought of as the young Apollo of before, there was a thoughtfulness and maturity in his face that became him well. The gaunt look and yellowness of skin would soon leave him when he had eaten a few more such dinners. She studied him covertly as he sat over his wine, for she had flatly refused to withdraw.

'Since I have not seen you for so long, and you make such a short visit, you cannot expect me to go and sit by myself, while you drink alone in here. You may pour me a glass of port, and I will keep you company.'

'If you were but a few years younger, aunt, I would need to look no further for a wife,' he said, complying with her request and raising his glass to her. 'You are so much more interesting than the young ladies.'

She frowned, but he could see that she was pleased. At the end of the evening she went to her chamber very thoughtful, and once her maid had divested her of her evening finery and brushed out her hair, she dismissed her and seated herself at her little writing desk.

'I shall not need you again tonight, and do not waken me too early tomorrow, for I have a letter I must write before I go to bed, and I am tired.'

'Would it not be better, my lady, to write in the morning?' The maid, who had been with her for years, was not afraid to remonstrate with her mistress.

'No, for I have in my mind just what I should say, and if I leave it to tomorrow I might not write at all.' For all that she hesitated many times in the writing, reading and rereading what she had put. When in the end she was satisfied she folded her letter, and inscribed on it the name of her god-daughter.

'I should not wish you to tell anyone what I have said,' she had written, 'but if the girl is as you say it seems to me that she might do very well. That she is outspoken and a tomboy would do her no harm in his eyes. It is too early for anything to be done, but I should wish you to bear in mind what I have said. If you are presenting the child later in the year, I shall come to London, and the introduction may be arranged.'

CHAPTER TWO

LADY CORNELIA, Countess of Pontesford, surveyed her eldest daughter with dissatisfaction.

'Harriet, I despair of you! You look the veriest hoyden. Your hair is coming down, you are covered with mud—even your face is muddy—and as for your petticoats...and you carry, I must tell you, a distinct odour of the farmyard. If it were even of the stable, it would not be so bad, but the farmyard, Harriet, unmistakably the farmyard!'

Lady Harriet hung her head. 'I am very sorry, Mama. I was at the stables with Papa, and he went on to the farm to see the new cows that have just come. And oh, Mama, they are very good! Of our own Sussex breed, of course, but far superior to our old stock, for their hinder ends, you know...' Her eager voice tailed off under her mother's affronted gaze.

'Really, Harriet, that you should think of mentioning such things, even to me! One would take you for the veriest farmer's daughter.'

'But I *am* a farmer's daughter, Mama,' murmured Harriet rebelliously.

'If the Earl, as a result of our financial misfortunes, takes an interest in the running of the Home Farm instead of busying himself in his rightful sphere, that is one thing. It is right that a land-owner should take an interest in his acres. If his interest leads him to lower himself by labouring among his tenants then that is his affair, and whatever my feelings I am silent,' she said inaccurately, but with sincerity.

'Yes, Mama, but . . .'

'Do not interrupt me, Harriet. I have not finished speaking. You, I am forced to remind you, are a young lady. At eighteen it is time you ceased careering round the countryside with your Papa. In only a few weeks from now you will be in London with me, preparing for your presentation at Court, although how that is to be managed now that St Erth has run up all those bills at Oxford, I do not know. Be that as it may, I am determined that you—and your sisters—are to have every chance. And heaven knows,' she added in parenthesis, 'you need it.'

It had to be admitted that Lady Harriet presented a discouraging sight to a mother who was unfortunate enough to be the parent of five daughters, and the wife of an impecunious husband. Of but medium stature, she looked small when seen against her mother's Junoesque build, to which the bearing of eight children, (of whom seven had survived infancy), had merely added a stately matronliness of deportment. Harriet's hair, though remarkably thick and long, was of an uninspiring shade of light brown. Her eyes, of an appealing pansy brown—like a spaniel's, said St Erth, with elder-brotherly frankness—were surmounted by a pair of strongly marked, straight eyebrows, that gave her face an unfashionably determined look, though they gave distinction to an otherwise unmemorable face. It was not that she was plain, for there was nothing amiss with any of her features, and her skin was good though a little tanned, even in winter, from the hours spent outside. But she would never be a beauty, and those eyebrows revealed more of her character than her Mama would have wished. While always intending to be good, and dutiful, Harriet was often in trouble for her wilful behaviour.

'And had you forgotten, Harriet, that you were to have accompanied me this afternoon when I went to call on Mrs Amberley?'

'I am very sorry, Mama,' repeated Harriet, who had in fact remembered perfectly well, and had taken her own measures to escape. Paying calls with Mama, when she was permitted to utter nothing but the merest banalities, was agony, in particular to Mrs Amberley, whose children were so overindulged that there was no preventing them from climbing all over one, and rifling through one's reticule.

Her unexpected docility softened Lady Cornelia's heart. She was not an unkind parent, and indeed well understood her eldest daughter's reluctance to grow up. But with Lady Amanda, at sixteen already bidding fair to become a beauty, she deemed it essential to launch Harriet into society before her sister was there to outshine her. She spoke more gently.

'Well, we will say no more about it, and indeed it was not a pleasant visit, as you may guess by my early return. Mrs Amberley's little Arabella was far from well, but had insisted on joining her mother in the drawing-room. She was so fretful that I took her on my knee, for Mrs Amberley has not the least notion of being firm with her, and persuaded her that she would be far better tucked up in her own bed. So she went, and I took my leave, for I could see that Mrs Amberley was longing to hang over her pillow, and drive her to a fever by stroking her, and asking her if she is not better every five minutes. But there—I should not speak so to you, for I am sure that Mrs Amberley is a good woman, and a devoted mother.'

'Yes, too devoted,' returned Harriet, reaching up to place a light kiss on her cheek. 'No, I have not made you dirty, dear Mama, and I am going instantly to change. How thankful I am that you are not such a mother!'

'It might have been better if I had been; at least, not exactly so devoted, but a little stricter,' replied Lady Cornelia severely. 'I sometimes think that I have allowed you far too much freedom. When you have changed your gown I expect you to spend at least half an hour practising that sonata. Then you should mend the really shocking rent I saw in your blue poplin last night.'

Washed, changed, and the sonata duly laboured over, Harriet repaired to the schoolroom. As she had expected she found not only the younger children but her other sisters there also, for the shabby old room was much cosier, in winter, than the draughty saloons downstairs.

Amanda, nearest to her in age, was embroidering a flounce, sitting gracefully in the wide window seat to get the best of the light. In the other window Edwina was hunched over a book, her fingers in her ears as she muttered Latin verbs to herself. Although only a year younger than Amanda, she was still childishly small and thin, and preferred boys' pursuits to the ladylike activities their mother thought appropriate. Their brother Harry, Viscount St Erth, at present up at Oxford, said admiringly that Eddy was cleverer than many of the other men of his year. This gave Lady Cornelia no pleasure at all.

The son born after Edwina had survived only three months, so the three younger children formed their own group, having little interest in their elders' lives at present. At twelve, Augusta was the ringleader in their games, loyally supported by the only other son of the house, Lord John. The baby of the family, seven-year-old Lady Isabella, struggled to keep up with them, and usually succeeded. They made a charming picture on the hearthrug before the fire guard, where they had mustered every toy soldier the nursery possessed to fight the Battle of Bala-clava. Owing to a shortage of soldiers, the Russians were represented by the inhabitants of the battered Noah's ark.

'Half a league, half a league, half a league!' chanted Lord John. 'No, not there, Bella. Put Mrs Noah over by the coal-skuttle.'

'For goodness' sake keep your voice down, John,' begged Edwina, raising a frowning face. 'I've only half an hour before tea, and I want to finish this page of verbs.'

'I don't know why you want to learn such prosy stuff when you don't have to,' replied her brother. 'I know I wouldn't. Anyway, it's our room more than yours. You're too old. Why don't you read in the library?'

'Because it's warmer here. And I'm not too old, be-cause I haven't put my hair up yet and don't go down to dinner like Harriet and Amanda. Besides, this is the schoolroom, so I'm the only one using it properly.' John, routed, returned defiantly to his chant, and Edwina scowled at him, pushed her fingers more firmly into her ears and resumed her studying. Lady Amanda lifted her cornflower blue eyes from her embroidery.

'Have you done your sonata?' she asked in her soft, pretty voice. 'We could hear Mama from here. Why did you not take the back stairs, so that you could at least have been changed before she saw you?'

'I know, I should have done, but I did not know she was returned. Did you go with her? It sounds a horrid after-noon.'

'No, I wanted to finish this flounce, and she said I might. Look, it is nearly done. Do you like it?'

'It is beautiful. How kind you are, Amanda. I wish it were you going to London instead of me.'

'Well, my turn will come soon, and I like to make pretty things. Besides, I shall be coming with you, so I shall have all the fun of shopping, and seeing all the sights. This Indian muslin is so lovely, you will look beautiful, and everyone will want to dance with you.'

'I don't suppose they'll even notice me. Not that I'd mind not dancing, exactly, but Mama will scold.'

'She wants you to get a husband,' put in Augusta pertly from the hearthrug. Her sisters rounded on her.

'Augusta! Have you no elegance of mind? A girl of your age should not be thinking of such things, let alone saying them.'

'It's true enough—though you shouldn't have said it, Gussie. I must try to marry well so that I can help the rest of you—not that you will need any help, Amanda. What a pity you aren't the eldest!'

'You won't need to help me. I shall be a soldier in a red coat, and fight the foe. Hurrah!'

'Oh, hush, Johnny, you do not know what you are saying,' begged Amanda. 'I am sure Mama will not expect you to marry anyone to whom you are not attached, Harriet.'

'No, but I cannot imagine finding myself attached to any man. I do not want to be married at all, just yet. I want to do something, to be something. If I were a man, I would be an explorer, or a doctor, or a farmer like Papa. Not just spend my time worrying about the servants, and the children, and my dresses.'

'I should like to be a married lady, and have a house of my own, and a dear little baby,' put in Isabella.

'Babies are all right, I suppose, but I'd rather have a foal, or a calf. Or even a pig, if it were a good one,' Harriet added reflectively. Amanda's shocked face and John's shout of laughter recalled her wandering mind. 'I dare say no one will ask for me, and I shall come home again, and be a comfort to Mama and Papa in their declining years.'

Even Amanda looked dubious about this, though she did not like to point out that the presence of their eldest daughter was unlikely to be a comfort to Mama, who showed as yet little sign of declining. Edwina had no such scruples.

'Much good that would be,' she said, laying down her Latin grammar and rising to wrest from John's arms the cushion which he had wrapped in an old shawl, and which he was rocking as he grunted, pig-like, to it. 'If I had been a boy, I'd have gone up to Oxford, like Harry, and tried for a Fellowship. We just have to make the best of it.'

'Yours not to reason why!' put in their irrepressible brother. 'Yours but to jolly well find a rich husband so that I can go into a good regiment!'

United against a common foe, his sisters set upon him with righteous wrath.

Later that evening, the Countess availed herself of her wifely privilege of visiting the Earl in his dressing room as he was arraying himself for dinner. After allowing him to tell her, at great length, about the excellence of his new cows, (for she was nothing if not diplomatic with him), she proceeded to implore him not to allow Harriet to accompany him so often to the farm. The Earl was surprised, and somewhat annoyed, for he enjoyed the company of his eldest daughter, and often admitted that her eye for a beast was nearly as good as his own.

'I can see no harm in it, my lady. She is always with me, and it is no more than she has always done.'

'I do not mean that there is any impropriety,' she explained patiently. 'Indeed, how could there be, if she is with you? I meant only that now that she is growing up, and becoming a young lady, she would be more properly employed indoors. It is time she gave up her childish ways.'

The Earl was inclined to be rebellious. 'It pleases me to have her accompany me.'

'Yes, indeed, and I would be the last to deny you such a pleasure. But think of the future, my dear. Would you wish that she spend the rest of her life as your companion? I think you love her too well to deny her the chance of a home and family of her own.'

This was a shrewd blow, and he felt it as such. Like most fathers, he found it hard to believe that his daughter, who but yesterday had been a child at his knee, should leave him for another man. Yet he, knowing her so well, knew that she would never be happy to stay in the nest for ever.

'I suppose you are right. If you insist on presenting her this year...'

'I do. I must. Oh, I make no disparagement of Harriet, she is a good girl, and well enough looking, but no man would look twice at her if Amanda were in the room. If she is to find a husband, it should be soon. By the by, while we are on the subject, I had a letter from my god-mother, Lady Beatrice, a few days ago.'

'Still alive, is she? I thought she died some years ago.'

'No, that was my other god-mother. Lady Beatrice writes that her great-nephew has just returned from the Crimea, and inherited a substantial property some miles from here. He is in want of a wife, it seems, and from things I have said to her in my letters Lady Beatrice is inclined to think that Harriet might be a suitable match.'

'You'll not succeed in arranging anything for Harriet, my lady. She knows her mind too well.'

'I would not attempt it. I have never approved of parents interfering unnecessarily in their children's marriage plans. No, it is merely a suggestion. Nothing is to be said, of course, to either party.'

'Ten to one nothing will come of it,' said the Earl.

CHAPTER THREE

COLD MARCH rain fell relentlessly as Sir Robert rode into the stableyard at Atherington Hall. He dismounted and led his mare into the stable where she was lovingly received by the boy he had recently taken on to help his elderly groom. As he did so he noticed with irritation that the gutters were overflowing, the water splashing on to a wooden lintel whose rotted appearance bore mute witness to previous outpourings. He looked up at the sagging gutter and the movement sent an icy trickle down the back of his neck. He cursed as he ran for the shelter of the Hall.

Here, at least, some modicum of comfort had been achieved. A huge fire burned in the stone fireplace of the entrance hall—plenty of dead wood for the gathering in the neglected plantations—and the carved oak furniture glowed with beeswax polish. Robert stripped off his dripping coat and went to stand before the fire. His former batman came in and without a word handed his master a glass of punch. Robert sniffed appreciatively at the odour of lemon and rum that rose with the steam.

'A good thought, Barton.'

'Thank you, Captain. Major, as I should say.' Robert smiled. Barton was intensely proud of his master's rank, earned during the war when the carnage among officers meant that a man might rise swiftly.

'Neither Captain nor Major any longer, Barton.'

'And thank God for it too, Captain. I'm afraid you'll have to put up with me mis-calling you, though, for I can't seem to get used to any other.'

'As long as you bring me another glass of punch, you may call me what you will, Barton. It is a dreadful day out there.'

Barton was swift to refill his glass, then knelt to remove his master's wet boots.

'A Mrs Stolford called while you was out, Captain. Left her card.'

Robert took the proffered piece of pasteboard and examined it with a grimace. 'That's the third this week, and how many since we arrived—seven, or eight? They know what this place is like, they must realise we are in no state to be entertaining. The house is practically falling down round our ears!'

'The lady said she didn't wish to stand on ceremony, Captain. Says you're welcome to take potluck with them any day. Says she thought you might like a bit of company, seeing as you're here all alone.'

Barton's face was impassive, but Robert knew him well. 'I'm much obliged to her! Did she come alone, or did she bring any of the—company—with her?'

'That she did, Captain. Three daughters, and oh, wasn't they just disappointed not to find you at home.' Robert grinned at the spirited falsetto and rolling eyes that his servant suddenly achieved. Barton was serious at once.

'Very neighbourly in this part of the country, so I've always heard, Captain.'

'A dashed sight too neighbourly for my taste! I might just as well have stayed in Bath. I haven't come here to be neighbourly—at least, not yet. It's a pity we're not likely to get any more snow by now, although this rain will make the roads impassable for a few days, I imagine. Mrs Stolford must be a determined woman. What ever can have possessed her to bring her daughters out on a day like this? Her coachman won't have thanked her for it.'

'It's my belief she had heard you were difficult to see, and came today on purpose, thinking you were bound to be indoors and she would catch you.'

'Is there no Mr Stolford? It seems odd for her to be making the first call.'

'A widow-lady, I understand, Captain.'

Robert finished his punch and slipped his feet into the shoes Barton had brought him. 'How are the workmen getting on?'

'They should finish putting in the new stove tomorrow, and that'll be the kitchen nearly done. After that they can start on the bathrooms, unless there's anything else you want them to do next?'

'No, the bathrooms next. I intend to make this place a marvel of modern comforts. It should not be necessary for hot water to be carried up morning and evening. We can't do any proper work on the roof until later in the year, though I must tell someone to repair the guttering on the stables. It's all but fallen off.'

Barton, covertly studying his master, was glad to see some colour returning to his face as the fire and the punch did their work. He had known Robert since childhood, his father having been groom to Robert's late father. They were much of an age, and during their time in the Crimea had grown remarkably close. Robert had implicit trust in his man's loyalty, and Barton, for his part, not only respected his master but felt for him the protective affection of one who has been a comrade in arms against a common enemy, be it human or medical. Robert had saved Barton's life in battle, and in his turn Barton had watched over him when he was wounded, braving doctors, superior officers and most courageously of all, Miss Nightingale herself.

They had been at Atherington Hall for over a month. Sir Robert had been welcomed almost with tears of joy by the superannuated couple who had struggled for years to keep at least part of the house habitable. They had done their best, but the years had taken their toll, and after one look at the damp, cobwebbed rooms Robert had summoned every able-bodied woman in the village and set them to cleaning. As he had foreseen, there was a great deal of expense. While he was not a poor man, the reasonable fortune his father had left him being safely invested in the City, he was not wanting to invest too much capital in something that would not pay. For the past weeks, now that work on the house was under way and could safely be left for Barton to oversee, he had been riding over his lands to see whether some of the burden of the expenditure could be borne by them.

He had been horrified by what he found. While he had known that the farms would not be in a good state, he had been unprepared for the dilapidation that met his eyes. Hedges were untrimmed and unlaid, full of gaps, and ditches silted up so that some fields were almost under water. The few fields under plough looked poor, and the pasture was full of docks and thistles. The few cattle that he saw were bony and miserable.

The farm buildings and cottages were worse. Several of the farmers were old men, worn down by the uneven struggle to keep their farms going with no help or support from their landlord. The labourers, too, were for the most part older, any young men having long since departed to look for a better life in the towns. The farmers brightened a little when he spoke vaguely of improvements, but at the back of their eyes he sensed a hopelessness, a shrinking from the effort involved and a fear of having their rents increased. One, a younger man, who had recently inherited the tenancy from his father, was a different matter. Surly at first, he had cheered almost at once when he sensed Robert's interest.

Nearly incoherent with excitement, he had taken his new landlord over every foot of the farm. Robert was slightly encouraged to see that here, at least, the hedges and fences were sounder, and some at least of the ditches were clean.

'I'd 'ave done more, sir, 'ad I the time and the money. This field, d'you see, she lies very 'eavy. She needs proper draining, then that 'ud be as sweet a pasture as you'd wish to see.'

Robert interrupted the flow. 'How is it that so little money was available? Were the rents so high? Did Sir Arthur allow nothing for repairs and improvements?'

Farmer Robins glanced doubtfully at him. 'He were never what you might call interested in the land, sir, even before 'e got to be so old and queer, if you'll pardon the word. He had a steward, a man called Studdock. Proper bad job 'e were. Rooked Sir Arthur left and right, and all the while talking to him so sweetly 'e'd charm the birds off the trees, as the saying goes. Reckon Sir Arthur never knew the rents was up, or that 'alf of them went into Studdock's pocket. As for repairs—well, you might as well ask for the moon.'

'What became of this Studdock?'

'He 'ung on as long as he could, but soon as 'e 'eard as Sir Arthur were dying, 'e were off. In the night, 'e went, and no one any the wiser. We'll not see 'im again in these parts, and thankful for it.'

'As you say, we're well rid of him. I had been minded to employ a steward myself, but I see I must be careful in my choice.'

'If I might make so bold, sir, will you not do the job yourself?'

'But I know nothing of farming, Robins. It should be someone who knows all the modern methods, the new ideas.'

'It needs more than that, sir. Modern methods won't do no good if nobody'll try 'em. It needs a man of education, sir, and a man used to giving orders, like in the Army, sir. They're used to going their own way round 'ere, by now. They'll not take kindly to change. But you're master round 'ere now, you can tell 'em. And what's more, they'll listen. You've no 'igh and mighty ways with you, sir, if you'll pardon the liberty, and I know as you'll listen to them, same as you've been listening to me. That's what it needs.' Robins wiped his brow, bedewed with sweat after one of the longest speeches he had ever made in his life.

Robert returned to his original objection. 'That's all very well, but haven't I just been telling you I know nothing about it all. I don't deny I'd like to take it on myself, for I want employment of some kind, but not if I can't do a proper job.'

'Well, sir, it seems to me it shouldn't be too 'ard just to learn it. There's books, and that.'

'Go back to school, you mean? I suppose I could. But I'd need a teacher, Robins. Reading isn't enough, for this. I'd need to *see* it done.'

Robins scratched his head thoughtfully. 'That's true sir. You wants to go somewhere not too far off, where the land's like our own. That'll need a bit of thought, that will. But you've not taken against the idea, then, sir?'

Robert considered. To his surprise, he found that his interest had been engaged. The last few weeks had shown him that he was happiest when he was busy. Restoring the old house, and improving it, had given him something to work at, and he had not been above rolling up his sleeves and pitching in with the workmen. But that was already coming to an end, and he needed something else to occupy his mind and his body. The prospect of learning lifted his spirits. To be doing something useful, and creative, to be involved in the creation of new life and bound to the cycle of the seasons. It was a good thought. He smiled. 'By damn, I'll do it. We'll make these the best farmed acres in Sussex!'

The farmer caught fire from his enthusiasm, and they parted much pleased with each other, and with many plans for the future. Now Robert was returning from another visit to Robins, and was wondering how Barton would take the scheme that they had hatched between them.

'Robins has come up with an idea for me, Barton. It seems that a cousin of his married a man who farms for the Earl of Pontesford. I've never met his lordship, but Robins says he has for some years been improving his lands, and trying out some of the modern methods. He's well thought of by his tenants, and, what is more important, since he is but thirty miles away his soil is much like we have here. I could learn a great deal from such a man, if I should make a stay with him and study his ways.'

'Very good, Captain. How long shall we be staying with his lordship?'

Robert cast a sidelong look at his man. 'You misunderstood me, Barton. When I spoke of staying with him, I referred not to the Earl but to his tenant, Robins's cousin's husband.'

Barton was moved to expostulate. 'A gentleman like you, sir, staying on a common farm! Whatever are you thinking of? If his lordship should come to hear of it, he would think it very odd.'

Used to his batman's outspoken character, Robert merely laughed. 'Oh, this is not a *common* farm, Barton: Robins assures me that it does *un*commonly well. I shall not be visiting as Sir Robert Atherington, but as plain Mr Roberts, a friend of Robins's who is wishful of learning about farming, and is not above helping out here and there in exchange for his instruction. Should his lordship come to hear of it there could be no possible objection, and he need never know who I am.'

'But what about me, Captain? You will not go without me, surely?'

Seeing that he was really hurt, Robert put his hand on Barton's arm, and shook it gently. 'Plain *Mr* Roberts does not travel with a manservant, my friend. And, besides, I need you here. Who is to oversee the work on the house if you come with me? There is no one else I can trust to see that all is done properly.'

Barton was mollified, but still regretful. 'I still think you ought to be staying with the Earl, Captain. What would people say?'

'Well, I trust they will say nothing, since nobody will know but us, and Robins. Frankly, I do not care much, so they may say what they will. What might be frowned on in plain Captain Atherington may, in Sir Robert Atherington, be more properly called mere eccentricity. I have no fears of being cast off by society, at least while I am still the possessor of my cousin's fortune!'

'But who will look after you? It will not be at all what you are accustomed to.'

Robert frowned slightly. 'Come, now, Barton, I am not a child. I am very well able to look after myself—at least for a while. As for what I am accustomed to, I am sure a homely farmhouse will be a paradise of comfort compared to what we experienced on the Crimea, or even compared to this place when we first arrived. It will at least be clean, I suppose! Lady Beatrice recommended fresh air and exercise for me, you know. While this may not have been precisely what she meant, I am persuaded that it will suit me very well. You know I am not anxious, as yet, to take my place in local society?' He glanced at his man, who nodded unwillingly. 'I need time, Barton, time to be myself, and to find out, if I can, just what sort of person "myself" is. I know that soon I must be Sir Robert, with all the responsibilities that entails, including, I suppose, a Lady Whoever Atherington and a nursery of little Honourables. That is my future. But for the moment I would like, just for a while, to be plain Mr Roberts of nowhere in particular. Can you understand that?'

Barton gave a nod. 'Reckon I can, Captain,' he said, gruffly but affectionately. 'Maybe you're right. You'll pardon me if I spoke out of turn.'

'Out of turn? Plain Mr Roberts doesn't know the meaning of the words,' Robert replied.

CHAPTER FOUR

HARRIET, DETERMINED to atone for the unmaidenly behaviour that had displeased Lady Cornelia, threw herself
into the preparations for her visit to London with dogged
determination. While she could not summon up any joy in
the prospect—indeed, she saw herself in gloomier moments as a sacrifice on the altar of family duty—she tried
at least to present a cheerful face to the world. It was not
always easy. She stood patiently for what felt like hours in
her mother's dressing-room while the dressmaker's cold
fingers pushed and tugged at gown after gown, and Lady
Cornelia and Amanda made suggestions. Amanda, indeed, showed more pleasure in the new clothes than her
sister, for as the beauty of the family she had always taken
more of an interest in fashion. While Harriet was feminine enough to delight in new gowns, the knowledge that
she was to wear them in a new and alarming place was
enough to destroy all her pleasure. Even Harriet felt some
interest, however, when a parcel from London arrived,
containing one of the new 'artificial crinolines' of which
few had even heard.

'I shall be grateful for ever to Cousin Alice,' announced Lady Cornelia. 'To manage to send us one so
quickly! I am sure most girls already in London have not
got one yet. You must sit down at once, Harriet, and write
her a letter of thanks.'

'Oh, Mama, she must try it on first,' begged Amanda. 'Only feel how light it is! I cannot believe it will hold the skirts out properly.'

'Very well, we shall try it.' Lady Cornelia, too, was eager to see the effect. 'Take off your outer petticoats, Harriet. Good gracious, child, surely you can lace your stays tighter than that? Minter, tighten Lady Harriet's stay laces, if you please.'

'I am sorry, Mama, but it is so uncomfortable. I cannot breathe properly when they are tight.'

'You would notice it less, my dear, if you wore them properly tightened every day. Do not think that I have not noticed that you lace them up properly only for the evening, or when we are trying on your new clothes.' Harriet blushed, for she had indeed hoped that this had not been apparent. 'Also, my dear, you would have more breath if you were to move in a calmer, more ladylike fashion. You are forever hurrying, and it is most unbecoming in a young lady to be hot and breathless as you often are.'

'Yes, Mama,' said Harriet, trying not to wince as her laces were mercilessly tightened by Minter.

'It is very important for the line, dearest,' said Amanda earnestly. 'With the longer waist, it is vital to have a smooth shape for the bodice to fit to.'

'Very true, my dear. When I was your age—before I met your Papa—I had a very tiny waist. At that time skirts were not so full, of course, and they were shorter, too, but such sleeves as we wore! I dare say you would laugh to see them, they were so big, but we thought them very fine. Only, of course, if one did not have a neat waist, one was inclined to look very large on top.'

Harriet, the lacing finished, was now bereft of speech. Wordlessly she stepped into the contraption that Amanda had placed carefully on the floor. It looked like nothing in the world so much as a collection of children's hoops, joined together by strips of fabric. Amanda carefully lifted up the top, and fastened it at the waist.

'How very droll you look, Harriet—like a birdcage!' Even Lady Cornelia had to smile at the odd appearance. Minter slipped a petticoat of fine cambric over her head, and followed it by one of rustling silk.

'Which gown shall I fetch, my lady?'

'Let it be the ball gown, Mama, the pink georgette with the layered skirt,' begged Amanda.

'Very well,' nodded Lady Cornelia.

The dress once fastened, Harriet shook out her skirts and took a few experimental steps.

'How pretty!' cried Amanda. 'Your skirts sway when you walk. How does it feel?'

'Very strange,' admitted Harriet, 'but pleasant. I feel so light! I shall hardly dare to go outside on a windy day, for fear I might blow away!'

'It is certainly a great improvement,' said Lady Cornelia, ignoring such levity. 'I should think you will feel the cold, though, without your thick petticoats. You must be sure to wear several underneath it, if the weather is cold. The skirts hang very much better, and, as you say, Amanda, the swaying of the skirt when you move is most graceful. I believe it might even improve your dancing, Harriet!'

Knowing that this was by way of a joke, Harriet gave a dutiful smile, but she blushed as well. The sad truth was that as a dancer she was a great disappointment to her mother. An instructor had been engaged, and now visited the house twice a week, to supplement the lessons all the girls had received since they were children. Amanda moved across the floor as lightly as thistledown, with no apparent effort, but Harriet seemed to have been born, said Lord John unkindly, with two left feet.

It was only by an effort of fierce concentration that Harriet was able to circle the floor without either stepping on her partner's feet of falling over her own. Counting in her mind—and occasionally in forgetful moments out loud—she would stiffly revolve, feeling more like an automaton than a human girl. Unfortunately the effort made her frown horribly, her dark eyebrows drawn almost into one continuous line across her face.

'My lady, my lady,' cried her despairing instructor, 'look up, my lady, and smile!' Harriet did so, and instantly missed her step. A flicker of anguish crossed the instructor's face as she lost her balance and trod heavily on his foot.

'It is no good, Amanda,' Harriet wailed to her sister when they were alone. 'I shall never be able to do it. If I can't even look up at my partner without getting into a muddle, how can I ever converse with him? I would cripple the poor man before we had even had time to agree what a pleasant ball it is, and how good the orchestra!'

These trials, however, paled into insignificance when it came to The Curtsy.

On being presented to Royalty, Harriet was required to sink into a deep curtsy, rise, and withdraw backwards. For this grand occasion she would be wearing a Court dress of more than usual splendour, which was to be purchased in London, since her mother did not trust a country dressmaker with so important a commission. Harriet, even dressed in an everyday dress with moderately narrow skirts and no train, proved constitutionally unable to perform the curtsy.

'I cannot understand it,' mourned Lady Cornelia to the Earl in the privacy of the marital bed. 'It is not as though she has poor balance.'

'Poor balance? I should think not!' responded her spouse. Why, the girl can stick on any horse in the stables, even that new colt of mine, Jupiter.'

'Unfortunately, our daughter may not be presented on horseback,' Lady Cornelia responded crossly, 'and I shall be obliged to you, my lord, if you will not encourage her to ride that half broken colt just as I am on the verge of taking her to London.'

'Very good, my dear.' The Earl was nothing if not reasonable, and he was a fond, though absentminded, father. 'Not that she'd come to a whit of harm, but just as you please.' He ruminated, punching thoughtfully at his pillow before laying his night-capped head on it. 'All the same,' he added, as he composed himself for sleep, 'it's a pity she can't appear on horseback. Appears to advantage, y'know. Got a good seat. Better than any of the others. Better than St Erth, even. Dashed if I've seen a better rider anywhere, for her age!' he finished, much struck.

Lady Cornelia sighed, but forbore to point out that having a good seat on a horse was worth little in what the Earl, with what she considered to be undue coarseness, had once referred to as 'the matrimonial stakes'.

Alas, the new hooped crinoline did nothing to improve Harriet's dancing. Nor, several days later, had she yet managed to rise from her curtsy without clutching for support. If anything, thought her mother with rising exasperation, she was worse. Voluntarily forgoing her usual rides to make time for more fittings and practices, she was looking pale, and there was a worried crease between what her mother privately thought of as her preposterous eyebrows.

'Do not, I implore you, frown so, Harriet,' snapped Lady Cornelia, as her eldest daughter, concentrating furiously, approached her at a stately pace and sank to the ground in her reverence. Distracted, Harriet looked up, wobbled, and at once sat down in a heap on the floor. Amanda put up her hand to cover a smile, for really her sister looked very funny, but Lady Cornelia was not amused. Words failed her and she covered her eyes with her hand, while Harriet scrambled to her feet.

'I am sorry, Mama, I truly am. I do try, but I don't seem able to manage it at all.' Near to tears, her voice wobbled, and her mother nobly refrained from scolding.

'I know you are trying, my dear. I am sure we can do it eventually. But just for now I am going to lie down for a little while.'

Much chastened, Harriet ran to open the door, then as her mother left the room with stately tread, sank into the nearest chair. 'What shall I do?' she mourned. 'Poor Mama, she is so kind, though I know I must be vexing her.'

'Don't worry,' said Amanda comfortably. 'All you require is practice. Come on, I'll help you.'

'If I were a boy, I'd run away to sea,' muttered Harriet with sudden rebellion.

'If you were a boy,' Amanda replied reasonably, 'you wouldn't be having to do all this.'

Harriet gave no answer, for there was none she could give. Sighing, she resumed her slow approach to the throne, and bent her aching knees in another curtsy. 'How I wish I didn't have to go to London,' she mourned, little thinking how quickly her wish was to be granted.

An uncomfortable evening ensued. Harriet sat almost silent during dinner, and the burden of conversation fell entirely on Amanda and Edwina. The latter had recently been coming down to dinner when the family was alone, as Lady Cornelia thought it time for her to be thinking of growing up, but it was considered by everyone to be a mixed blessing. While she had a ready tongue, and at times a quick wit, her intelligence made her incline towards the erudite, which suited neither of her parents. Lady Cornelia, because she felt it was not suitable for a young girl to take such an interest in scientific subjects, and the Earl because, as he said, he could not understand what the deuce the girl was on about.

On this occasion a chance remark by her father had seduced Edwina into a dissertation about the skeleton of the giant lizard, recently named *Stegosaurus*, that had been discovered not long since. In vain did the Countess frown, and Amanda attempt to change the conversation.

'For my part,' said the Earl placidly, when she finally ceased, 'I cannot see why anyone should be interested in something that died all those hundreds of years ago.'

'Not hundreds, Papa, thousands!' corrected Edwina.

'Thousands, then. Mean to say, all over and done with now, eh? If it were a new breed of pig, that'd be a different matter, eh, Harriet?'

Harriet only hung her head, knowing that such a remark would vex her mother as much as Edwina's lecture.

'Speaking of new breeds, this is a very fine piece of mutton Cook has sent up. One of our own, of course,' he added complacently. 'May I carve you a slice, my dear? It is done to a turn.'

Lady Cornelia pressed her handkerchief to her lips. 'No, thank you,' she replied shortly.

'Dash it all, you've eaten nothing. Are you not well, my lady?'

'Mama had the headache this afternoon,' said Amanda, rising. 'Are you still in pain, Mama?'

'Thank you, Amanda. I must admit that my headache is worse rather than better. I think I will retire now.' She left the room, leaning on Amanda's arm.

Harriet was dismayed. 'Oh, Papa, it is all my fault! Mama never gets headaches like this in the usual way of things. I was so stupid and clumsy this afternoon, and annoyed Mama dreadfully. That must have brought it on.'

'Nonsense, my dear. A night's sleep and she'll be as right as rain, just you see.'

The Earl's optimism proved to be ill founded. The Countess passed a very indifferent night, unable to sleep for the pain in her head and eyes. In the morning she was unable to rise, and confessed that she found herself far from well. The doctor was sent for, in spite of her protests, for she was so rarely ill that she herself could not accept the possibility. The Earl over-rode her protests, however, for he was alarmed by her appearance.

The doctor took one look at Lady Cornelia, noted the redness of her eyes and the beginning of a rash on her skin, and came to an immediate diagnosis.

'Has your ladyship visited Mrs Amberley recently?'

Minter, hovering jealously over her lady, answered for her. 'Her ladyship visited Mrs Amberley just more than a week ago.'

'Then I very much regret to inform your ladyship that you have contracted the measles. Little Arabella Amberley has been full of them for several days.'

'I held the child on my knee, because she was fretful,' Lady Cornelia remembered. A terrible thought struck her. 'I know Amanda caught it when she was a child, and the others too, but Harriet? I do not believe she did!'

'No, my lady,' said Minter grimly. 'They all had it, but Lady Harriet was staying with her grandmama, and missed it.'

'At all costs you must keep her away from me,' ordered Lady Cornelia. 'I cannot have her taking the measles now! Pray heaven she has not already contracted it from me. I was with her only a short time today, and yesterday very little also. If she should catch it we should be undone, for you know, Doctor, that although she is rarely ill she takes things very badly when she is. After all my work, she would miss the Season, or at least look so washed-out that I would not be able to show her anywhere!'

Tears of weakness came into her eyes as she spoke. The doctor, who was an old friend, took her hand and patted it soothigly.

'There, now, it will be time enough to worry when we find she had taken it! Ten to one she will not do so, and I tell you straight, your ladyship, that you do yourself no good by worrying. It is of no use preserving Lady Harriet from the measles if you are too unwell to care for her! Let your good Minter nurse you, and Lady Amanda if you like, but above all keep yourself quiet and calm. I will send up a draught that will help you to sleep, and a lotion for the rash.'

Lady Cornelia had too much sense not to admit that he was right, but re-iterated her request that Harriet was not to enter the room, nor was she to spend time with her sister if she should help with the nursing.

'Let her be outside as much as she wills,' she said weakly, with the vague idea that her daughter would thus be stronger to fight off infection. 'She must not catch it, at all costs!'

CHAPTER FIVE

HARRIET'S DAYS underwent a metamorphosis. The visit to London being postponed indefinitely there were no more fittings, no more dancing and practising of her presentation. Forbidden by Lady Cornelia's strict edict she was banished from her mother's sickroom, and the burden of the nursing fell upon Amanda, who spent most of her time there. The attack, though uncomfortable, was not serious, and the doctor was sanguine that her ladyship would soon be recovered. For the moment, however, she had to be content to remain in bed, her eyes protected by drawn curtains and a red shade to the lamp.

Amanda's time was fully taken up with reading aloud, the administration of soothing draughts, and the bathing of prickly skin. Her mother sent her out each day to walk in the garden for air and exercise, but even then Harriet was not allowed to be with her sister. Bereft of her company, Harriet went to the schoolroom. She could not be there, however, during the children's lessons, and at other times she found it hard to join in their play or take an interest in Edwina's studies. An irrational feeling of guilt that her conduct had somehow been responsible for her mother's illness prevented her from riding round the farms with the Earl, and she formed the habit of taking long walks, accompanied only by one of the many dogs her father habitually kept.

The weather smiled, and April came in with unexpected warmth. Harriet could not stay within doors when the sun shone, when the new grass sprouted its deliciously fresh green and there were primroses and violets to be found on the banks. Her mother might perhaps not have been completely in approval of such solitary walks, but within the confines of their own land Harriet knew that her father, for one, would not object. The estate workers and farm people had all known her since childhood, and with True for company, she roamed happily through woods and fields. Her father noted with approval that the colour had returned to her cheeks, and told his wife that Harriet, far from taking her mother's illness, was in better looks than before. Lady Cornelia, still confined to her room, could only be glad to hear it.

Comfortably, if shabbily, clad in an old brown dress of worn dimity, with an unfashionable but warm woollen shawl round her for warmth, Harriet wandered through the lanes near the Home Farm. Her boots were muddy, as were the hems of her dress and petticoats, for she had been visiting the sheep and their new lambs. Her bonnet hung by its strings round her neck, and her hair, hastily twisted up and insecurely fastened, was slipping in loose coils to her shoulders. Lady Cornelia would have been extremely cross, but Harriet reasoned that there was no one to see her, and there was time enough to worry about her appearance when she was in London. A small bunch of sweet violets for the sickroom was clutched in one regrettably muddy hand, and she was humming as she strode in an unladylike fashion along the narrow sunken lane.

A warning shout and the sound of hoofs alerted her, and she looked hastily round. Tail stuck up in the air, head tossing with excitement, a well-grown dairy shorthorn heifer was galloping towards her. The lane was narrow and the hedges high, so there was no escape that way, and besides, the heifer should be stopped. Two steps took Harriet to a gate, and with one neat movement she unhooked it and opened it so that it blocked the lane. The heifer seemed to measure it with her eye. Harriet knew she was wondering whether to jump the gate, a feat which she knew was perfectly possible, and continue this enjoyable gallop. Fortunately the lure of the new grass in the field was tempting, and her cry and wave of her free arm decided the issue. The heifer swerved into the field and Harriet shut the gate.

As she did so, she was aware of a tall man running towards her. His clothes were stained with mud all down one side, and he was clasping his shoulder with one hand as he ran. His face was pale under an outdoors tan. She assumed that he was a new farm worker, as she did not know him, and thought vaguely that his clothes were of good quality for such a man.

'It is all right,' she called. 'She is safe in here, for there is no other gate out of this field, and the hedges are too high for her to jump.'

The man spoke in an unexpectedly cultured voice. 'That was well done! I am sorry if you were frightened, miss. She was gone before I knew it, and I couldn't even run after her for fear of scaring her more.'

'I didn't have time to be frightened. I knew she meant no harm, anyway.'

His face twisted into a wry grin, and she noticed with surprise that he was very handsome.

'No harm, indeed! She had me over in the mire the minute she was through the gate, wretched creature!'

'Perhaps something startled her. She's Johnson's Cowslip, isn't she? How do you come to be with her? Have you just started work on the farm? I did not know he had taken on anyone new.'

'Yes, in a manner of speaking. Does my inexperience show so much?'

'No.' She blushed slightly, fearful of having given offence. 'It is just that I know all the people at the farm.'

'I have been here just over two weeks. Farmer Johnson has kindly agreed to teach me some of his trade. I am to stay with him for some months, help with the work, and learn as I go. I don't do him much credit as yet,' he finished ruefully, rubbing again at his shoulder.

'Oh, you are hurt!'

'It is nothing. An old wound that I jarred when I fell.' He spoke roughly, and she sensed his unwillingness to be fussed over.

'Well, you are a soldier, I collect, and I know how brave they are, so I will say no more! And now you are to be a farmer. Shall you like it, do you think?'

'Above all things I had no idea, before I came here, how interesting it all is. I thought it was simple stuff, you know, but I find I might as well be back at school.'

'Yes, indeed. Papa says that it should be possible to study farming at the Universities, instead of Classics. My brother thought it very droll, and threatened to tell his tutor that he wished to study agriculture instead of Aristotle!'

'A strange thought indeed. I imagine the worthy tutor might not take too kindly to such a remark, though now I am inclined to think that such a study might benefit a man much more.'

Harriet gave a little giggle. It struck Robert all at once how different her giggle was from that of the young girls he had met in society. He thought that in spite of her unprepossessing appearance she had a pleasant character. He liked the directness of her questions, and the lack of shyness with which she spoke and looked at him. She was obviously a lady, but she displayed none of the false modesty that he had come to expect from the young women he had before encountered. Harriet, for her part, did not know quite what to make of him. His clothes, though better than a farm worker might have been expected to wear, were plainly made and well worn, and the fact that he was working for Johnson did not indicate a gentleman. Yet his speech and manners were those of polite society. In a drawing-room she could never have questioned him, and would probably have been quite tongue-tied in the face of such a good-looking man, but out on the estate she was used to talking to her father's tenants, and she took it for granted that she had a right to ask questions.

'You do not sound quite like a soldier, nor yet a farmer,' she remarked enquiringly. Robert was reminded that he must keep to his persona.

'My father had me sent to the best school he could afford, miss,' he said. This was indeed true. His father had sent him to Eton.

'Is he a farmer?'

'Oh, no, miss. He was, er, in business. My cousin has recently left me some land, and I was minded to turn farmer.'

'Well, you could not do better than to learn from Johnson. He is an excellent choice of teacher.'

'He will think me a poor pupil for this day's work.' He glanced at the heifer, who had her head down and was grazing peacefully, with the air of one who has never dreamed of galloping. 'I only had to take her down to...that is...' He paused in embarrassment.

Harriet came to his rescue. 'You were taking her down to the bull, I suppose,' she said calmly, casting a knowledgeable eye over the switching tail.

He was relieved, and a little surprised. He had taken her for the daughter of some well-to-do local squire, but now thought that she must come from one of the farming families of the area. 'Yes, I was. She's Mr Johnson's pride and joy, excepting only the new Sussex cows that have just been bought. How he will roast me when I tell him I was bettered by her!'

'We had best get her down to the bull before you tell him,' she decided practically. 'Have you a halter for her?'

'Yes. I thought I had it on her but it cannot have been properly done, for she slipped her head out of it when she knocked me flying. It must be lying in the mud over there.'

'Then True shall fetch it for you. Here, True!' The dog, which had been sitting quietly on the bank, came to her call with tail waving. 'Fetch it, True! Fetch it!'

'Will she do so?' asked Robert as the dog darted off.

'Oh, yes, she is very clever. My brother Harry spent all last summer training her. It became quite a game—for him to leave things hidden for her to find and bring back to him. She will be grateful to you for giving her a chance to show off her trick—see how proud of herself she is!' And indeed the dog, approaching, was wagging her tail furiously and grinning round a mouthful of the rope halter that she was trailing behind her.

Robert laughed.

'Good girl! Yes, you are a good girl. No, there is nothing else for you to fetch just now, so there is no use looking at me so appealingly!' Harriet made to take the halter, but he would not permit her.

'I am muddy already, but you must not touch it—it is filthy, miss ... forgive me, I cannot keep calling you miss. May I be permitted to know your name?'

Harriet blushed slightly. It had not occurred to her that he would not know who she was. 'I am Harriet Milborne.'

'Miss Milborne, then. And I am Robert ... er, Roberts, that is.'

Harriet's blush deepened. 'I am not Miss Milborne,' she said in a small voice.

'I beg your pardon ... I should have thought ... Mrs Milborne, I suppose. Only you seemed so young...' It was his turn to blush. Harriet hastened to put him right.

'Oh, no, I am not married! I should more properly have said, I am Lady Harriet Milborne. My father is the Earl of Pontesford.'

Robert was startled. 'Lady Harriet! I can only beg your pardon, my lady. But to meet you here alone, unguarded ... I never thought ...'

'I must own it is not quite what my mother would like, though Papa never has any objections so long as I stay on our own land, for I know everyone here, and they know me. Until I met you!'

The brown eyes she raised to his face were completely free from coquetry. He thought how refreshing it was to meet a young lady who did not try to attract him, then remembered with a shock that in her eyes he was not to be classed in the group of men with whom she might be inclined to flirt. He wondered a little bitterly if she even saw him as a man at all. Many people of her class, he knew, considered working men and women as somehow slightly less than human. Unfairly piqued, he bowed to her as subserviently as he knew how.

'I thank you for your help, your ladyship. I hope my presence has not disturbed your walk.'

Harriet was hurt, but not offended. 'I am afraid I should have told you sooner. I did not mean to mislead you, and I know I do not look like an Earl's daughter, for my mother is always telling me so. I suppose you will not let me help you catch the heifer now, though I am afraid Farmer Johnson will be annoyed if she does not get to the bull this afternoon.'

He was melted at once. 'If I may make so bold, I find both your appearance and your conduct the epitome of a true lady.' He had his reward, for the brown eyes were once again raised to his in friendliness.

'How very pretty—and I am afraid quite untrue, though I am grateful that you should say it. If you were to see the young ladies of society in London, you would know that I do not compare to them either in looks or behaviour.'

Robert, who had seen plenty such ladies, was inclined to agree with her, though not for worlds would he have hurt her feelings again by saying so. 'If you can indeed help me to catch this wretched creature, I shall consider you the most gracious lady under the sun.'

'Then you must give me the halter, muddy or not. You shall see that, though I am a lady, I am not altogether useless!'

Hiding the halter behind her skirts, and bidding him stay by the gate, she softly approached the grazing animal. Talking gently, she reached out her free hand and began to scratch her back, at the top of her tail. The heifer looked at her, decided she was harmless, and continued to graze. Still scratching, Harriet moved her hand slowly up the back until she was standing by the shoulders. Without making any sudden movements she reached into her pocket and came out with a handful of oats, which she dropped on the grass in front of the heifer's nose. Eager for the treat the animal sniffed at them, stretching out an experimental tongue. While she was occupied, Harriet gently slipped the halter over her horns and, when she raised her head, under her jaw.

For a moment Robert held his breath as it looked as though the heifer might set off at a gallop again. But as Harriet continued to talk, and as she was anyway now much calmer, she decided to give in and accept the rope. In triumph, Harriet led her to the gate.

'Lady Harriet,' breathed Robert in awe, 'you should have been a duchess!'

CHAPTER SIX

As Harriet walked home she felt more cheerful than she had done for many weeks. It had been so pleasant, she thought, to prove that she could perform a useful task. She almost regretted that she had revealed her rank, but a moment's thought told her that it was a secret that could not have been kept for more than a day, since everyone else knew her only too well. She did not pause to contemplate the nature of her feelings. She only knew that she had found a friend, someone with whom she could feel at ease. She looked no further than the immediate future. Whatever happened later, she had some days of happiness to look forward to.

Robert, for his part, was surprised to find that for the rest of the day his thoughts kept straying to the Earl's unlikely daughter. He liked the openness of her manner, and was impressed by her quick-witted reactions when faced with a crisis. Most young ladies he had ever met, he thought, would have been more inclined to succumb to strong hysterics when faced by a runaway heifer. She was nothing to look at, of course, though her eyes were appealing. He thought that it would be pleasant to talk to her again.

The following afternoon Harriet, finding that she was not required either in the sickroom or in the schoolroom, took herself off for another walk. Without inquiring too closely into her own motives she decided to visit Mrs

Johnson at the farm. She found that good lady turning her cheeses in the dairy, and was warmly welcomed. She made her compliments on the number and appearance of the cheeses, which glowed like golden suns on the stone shelves.

'Yes, I'm pleased with them this year,' admitted Mrs Johnson, running a complacent eye over them and pausing to check on the cream rising in the pans. 'The cows have given so well, this spring. Since the pastures were drained we can put them out weeks earlier, and the grass really gets the milk flowing. How surprised my mother would have been, to see so many cheeses already out of the moulds, and it only April yet! She never reckoned on having one out till May, for there's no milk without grass, and that's a fact. Will you come into the house, m'lady, and take a drink of milk, and a piece of my cake?'

'Thank you, Mrs Johnson, but I do not want to keep you if you are busy.'

'Bless you, my dear—my lady, I should say—it's always a pleasure to see you here. I remember you coming to see me when you were so little I had to lift you up so you could see into the cream pans, and it hardly seems but yesterday at that. And now we have some extra help staying with us, as you may not know, so I'm properly beforehand with everything. But I must ask you, how is her ladyship? What does the doctor say?'

Harriet was disappointed at the turn in the conversation, but replied politely as she preceded her hostess into the big stone flagged kitchen.

'She is not very ill, and we do not anticipate any danger. But she is very pulled down, and rather uncomfortable, I am afraid. She will not let me near her, for I have not had the measles.'

'She's lucky, then, for these things can be nasty when older people take them. The wonder is that she did not have it sooner, but there, you never can tell. And she'll be anxious to keep you in your best looks for your coming out. What a disappointment for you, that you've not left for London yet! But it will soon go by, and then you will be dancing the night away, as the saying goes!'

Harriet agreed rather wanly, but luckily the farmer's wife put this down to disappointment rather than a lack of interest in the pleasures to come. She patted Harriet's hand consolingly and pressed another slice of cake on her. Harriet felt that she could now bring the subject back to what she wanted to talk about.

'I am glad to hear that you have more help now, Mrs Johnson. I know how busy you have been since your Bessie was married.'

'That reminds me, m'lady—whatever do you think? Our Bessie is in the family way, and I'm to be a granny before the year is out!'

With the ready sympathy that always endeared her to the local people Harriet responded warmly, inwardly resigning herself to the mass of speculation, plans and memories that the news summoned up in Mrs Johnson's motherly breast. Her patience was rewarded, for at length that lady, catching sight of Robert approaching across the yard, paused to say,

'Here is the gentleman I was speaking of earlier, when I said we had more help. My cousin over by Uckfield sent him to us. It seems he's come into a bit of land and wants to farm it for himself, so Cousin said if he wanted to learn he couldn't do better than come to Johnson. And right he is too, though it wouldn't do to say it to his face, but he's as good a farmer as any hereabouts, and better than most.'

'I have often heard my father say that Johnson is the most knowledgeable farmer he had ever met, and not only that, but one who was prepared to try out new ideas, which is much rarer! I know how he respects his opinion.'

Mrs Johnson coloured with pleasure. 'Well, and I'm sure we couldn't have a better landlord, for his Lordship is always ready to encourage Johnson, when he gets one of his notions.'

Harriet gave a gentle nudge to the conversation. 'Your visitor is a friend of your cousin, you said?'

'Yes, and quite the gentleman too,' nodded Mrs Johnson proudly. 'He may dress in old clothes, but they're good quality, and his linen . . . I was in good service before I was wed, as well you know, and I know good linen when I see it. I did wonder whether he's maybe suffered a misfortune and come down in the world. He doesn't say a lot about himself. Not that he's all high in his ways. Very polite, he is, and prettily spoken. Now, see, you shall meet him, for he's coming to the house.'

Coming into the shady kitchen after the bright April sunshine, Robert did not at first perceive Harriet sitting quietly at the table.

Mrs Johnson bustled forward. 'Mr Roberts, here is Lady Harriet come to visit. I have been telling her about you.'

Robert looked quizzically at Harriet, who returned his look calmly. She was suddenly glad that she had subdued the impulse to put on a more becoming dress, and was dressed as she had been the day before—though rather less muddy. He started to raise his hand to his head in the countryman's gesture of respect, but Harriet rose and held out her hand.

'Good afternoon, Mr Roberts. I have not yet had time to tell Mrs Johnson that we have already met.'

Mrs Johnson glanced sharply at him, for he had not mentioned the fact to her. Robert smiled as he shook the proffered hand.

'Ah, I had hoped to hide my incompetence, but you have betrayed me, my lady! Lady Harriet came to my rescue with Cowslip yesterday, ma'am. But for her, the creature would have galloped half way to Horsham, and I should never have been able to face Mr Johnson again!'

Mrs Johnson laughed. 'He do love that animal, and no mistake. Will you have a drink of ale, or a piece of my cake, Mr Roberts?'

'No, thank you, Mrs Johnson. I know you are trying to fatten me up, but another mouthful after that mid-day meal you gave us is more than I can manage! I came only to tell you that the mare has foaled at last. A fine little filly, mother and baby doing well.'

'There, now, that is good news. Johnson will be pleased it wasn't another colt. Perhaps Lady Harriet would like to see them?'

'Thank you, Mrs Johnson, I should love to. She is in the loose box?'

'Yes, my lady,' he replied. 'Will you come, Mrs Johnson?'

'No, I've plenty to be getting on with; I'll see her later. Do you escort her ladyship and show her the foal.' Mrs Johnson's romantic mind had seized on the notion that Robert was a gentleman fallen from fortune, and who knew but what a timely marriage might restore those same fortunes, though it was well known that the Earl had but little money. Still, an Earl was an Earl, when all was said and done. No more than Lady Cornelia did she expect Harriet to marry well, for fond of her though she was, she was a little dab of a thing, in her eyes.

Harriet and Robert walked across the yard.

'I am sorry I betrayed your secret,' ventured Harriet. 'Farmer Johnson would not really have been cross, would he? I have always thought him a mild-tempered man.'

'Indeed he is, and very patient with my inexperience. No, it was for your sake I was quiet.' She looked up, surprised. 'It is not at all the thing for you to be spending time with a strange man, with no companion to lend you countenance,' he explained gently.

She sighed. 'I had True,' she offered. He smiled.

'Hardly admissible as a chaperon, I am afraid! A young lady about to make her come-out cannot be too careful of her reputation.' Good heavens, he thought, I sound like someone's maiden aunt!

'Yes, Grandmama,' she replied meekly, twinkling up at him.

He laughed. 'That is just what I was thinking! But you know I am right. Did you tell your parents that you had met me?'

'I am not allowed to see Mama while she has the measles, for fear of catching them,' she prevaricated. He raised an eyebrow. 'Well, I suppose she would not be best pleased. But Mrs Johnson says you are a gentleman, so I am sure it is all right.'

'Far from it, I am afraid—it makes it worse. If I were in truth a cowman, or a groom, no one would give it a second thought. I would be, as it were, outside the pale, not really a man.' She gave a gesture of protest. 'It is so, and you know it.'

Harriet could not deny that he spoke the truth, and chose to change the subject. They had by that time reached the door of the loose box, and she looked over the half door. 'Here is the foal. How lovely!' They were both silent in contemplation of the newborn animal, balancing on spindly legs to nuzzle at its dam. 'Each time it is like a miracle,' she said softly. 'I could never be tired of seeing it.'

He nodded. The mare lowered her head to lick the still wet coat of her baby.

'A new life. It is a wonderful thing, after what I have seen in the past two years.'

She responded instantly to the pain in his voice. 'It was very terrible, wasn't it? Mama would not permit us to read the newspaper reports, but my brother told me. I am so sorry for you—for all of you.'

To his surprise, he found himself able to talk of it. His eyes fixed on the foal, the girl beside him almost forgotten, the words poured from him. It was the first time he had consciously allowed his mind to go back to the war. The pictures he still saw in his dreams rose before his eyes, his voice grew hoarse as he poured it all out. The incompetence, the needless suffering and death, his own inability to help his men, he told it all without sparing the details.

At last he stopped. He felt drained, almost cleansed. Harriet was silent and he saw that her hands were clenched on the stable door, the knuckles white as she clung to it for support. She gave a gasping sob, and he saw that tears were pouring down her whitened cheeks.

'Lady Harriet! My God, what have I done! Forgive me, I should never have spoken of it to you. I do not know what made me do it.' He led her to a truss of clean straw and obliged her to sit on it, fishing in his pocket for a handkerchief when he saw her ineffectual search for her own. She blew her nose fiercely and struggled for composure.

'You should not ask for forgiveness. I am glad the you told me.'

He scarcely heard her. 'It was unforgivable! A young, sheltered girl like you, to have her ears sullied with such things. I deserve to be shot.'

She turned on him fiercely. 'Sheltered! Yes, I am sheltered, but why should I be? Why should not I be allowed to see what the world is really like? It hurts, yes. It is agony to think what has been suffered by men like you. But why should I be spared? I want to be a person, not a doll. I am proud that you should tell me.' Her face was pale and blotched with tears. She could not have looked less beautiful, but he was profoundly moved. The truth was that while he had been speaking he had forgotten who was with him. The contrast between this peaceful scene of creation and the slaughter he had known had been so telling that he would have blurted his thoughts out to anyone who had happened to be near. Nevertheless, now that it had happened, he found that he was glad that she had been the unwitting hearer.

'You shame me by your courage. I would give anything to be able to forget it all. It haunts my dreams.' The admission of weakness was hard, but it was the only gift he could make to her.

Her eyes shone with tears that she brushed impatiently away. 'Maybe, with time, the memories will become easier to bear.'

'I think that by telling you it is already less dreadful,' he said in wonder. 'I have not been able to speak of it until now.'

'I think it would not have mattered whom you told,' she said with more perception than he had given her credit for. 'I just happened to be here. I am glad, though, that it was I.'

'So am I.'

She rose and he followed suit. Looking up she smiled happily. 'So you will not preach propriety any more, Grandmama! We shall be friends, shall we not?'

He smiled back. 'We shall be friends. But very discreet friends. Now here is Mrs Johnson coming to see what we can be talking about so earnestly, so I will bow, my lady, and you shall carry on with your walk. We working men cannot be standing idle, you know.'

With a called farewell to the farmer's wife, Harriet did as she was bid. As she walked home, she felt that she had somehow become a new person. It was not that he had trusted her, for as she had perceived he spoke simply out of his own need, unconscious of her. Her life, like most girls of her class and age, had been safe, sheltered by her parents' care. That care had been as it were the walls and ramparts of her existence, keeping out all thoughts of the danger and sorrow of the everyday world. But of late she had begun to feel that while the walls kept unpleasantness at bay, they also kept her in. She was far from resenting her parents' love, but deep within her she had acknowledged a feeling that it was time for those walls to crack, for the light of day to be allowed in. As a young plant is nurtured by the gardener so she had grown, but now she was ready to blossom forth, to grow and give promise of the harvest of life to come.

CHAPTER SEVEN

THE APRIL days slipped by like a dream of spring. Lady Cornelia kept to her room, and Harriet continued to take her daily solitary walks. Sometimes she and Robert met by chance when she found him at work with the other men, and then they could exchange only a smile and a few words, though this was enough to light up her day. More often, though, they met as if by chance in a secluded part of the woods. An old hammerpond gave back the clear blue of the sky, and under the trees the grass was thick with the juicy spears of unopened bluebells, and drifts of delicate wild anemones.

Here they could sit on a fallen log, and talk. Sometimes when she returned home Harriet could scarcely remember what they had spoken of. Robert told her of his time in the Crimea—but more gently now, without the fierce urgency of his first outrush of words. Harriet made him laugh with tales of her family, simple things that had no great significance, but which taught him to understand her thoughts and feelings.

Lost in her idyll, Harriet did not know that she glowed with happiness. Lady Cornelia would have been instantly suspicious, Amanda would have noticed at once, but they did not see her. Certainly Edwina, blind to anything outside the covers of a book, was oblivious to her sister's shining eyes. The Earl, who would at once have detected the slightest change in appearance in one of his horses, was blind to his daughter's looks, thinking only that the fresh air was doing her good.

Robert confided his plans, in a simplified form, to Harriet. 'I want to make the best of this land. It's been shockingly neglected for many years. My cousin took no interest in it at all.'

'Why was that? It seems such a terrible waste.'

'I am afraid the truth is he was a dreadful miser. He once turned his own sister from the door when she came to visit. Said he had no food in the house, and if he let her in, he would be obliged to send out for some!'

'Poor woman! Was she very much upset?'

'I do not think so. From what I have heard she was nearly as bad as he, and only went to see whether he had anything worth leaving, and whether it was worth making up to him for a mention in his will.'

'That is not a respectful way to speak of your relations.' Her prim tone was belied by the twinkle in her eyes.

'No, indeed, how shocking! What must you think of me!'

'Why, that some of your relations are nearly as peculiar as mine! I have a cousin in Scotland who is firmly convinced that she is the reincarnation of Mary Queen of Scots,' she informed him.

'Well, that is a trifle odd, to be sure, but quite harmless.'

'Yes, but she also claims that her dog is the reincarnation of Mary Queen of Scots's dog, and,' she continued with the air of one bringing out a trump card, 'she carries on all her correspondence in Gaelic!'

He gave a shout of laughter that sent a nearby duck squawking in alarm from her perambulations by the pond. 'I don't believe it! You are roasting me.'

'Not at all. The result is, of course, that nobody ever answers her letters, and her man of business is in despair.' She smiled with pleasure to see him laugh. 'It is not even very consistent, for Edwina says that Mary would more probably have corresponded in French, and that is the sort of thing she knows. The cream of it is, my cousin is not even Scottish. She comes from Essex.'

'Enough!' He wiped his streaming eyes. 'I concede defeat. Alas, Cousin Arthur was no more than a common or garden skinflint.'

'Yes, in this contest I think I have the better of you. Still, we should be thankful that he was. If he had left his land in good heart, you would never have come here, and we should not have met.'

'No, I suppose I should just have continued where he left off. I am glad that he behaved as he did—not just because I have come here, though I am glad I did, but because it gives me a chance to make something out of nothing. That is what I need, a purpose in life. To see the land productive, the working men content and prosperous...'

'You will have men working for you, then?'

'Some few, at least,' he prevaricated, concealing once again the fact that the few tens of acres she supposed him to have inherited was in fact nearer a thousand, comprising plenty of woodland as well as the cultivated. He regretted now that he had not told her the truth from the first. A perverse streak of pride had made him value the fact that she liked him for himself, not for his possessions. He knew by now that the Earl was far from being a wealthy man, and that with several daughters to marry off the countess would have welcomed his advent with open arms, particularly if he showed an interest in her eldest, less marriageable, daughter. The trouble was that as time went by it became more and more difficult to admit the deception, and he feared that Harriet's open and candid mind would withdraw from the evidence of his charade. He had no idea how he would extricate himself from this fix, for by now he had determined to continue the friendship, even if it meant going to London when she did. Like her, he was enjoying the golden moments, putting away from him all thoughts of the future and what it might bring.

'I envy you the chance of being active, and useful,' said Harriet wistfully. 'I suppose the nearest I will ever get to it is helping Papa on the estate, and that is not much. When I go to London I shall not be able to do even that.'

'It is talked of again, then?' He was surprised at the pang the idea caused him.

'Yes, Mama will soon be downstairs again. Everything is prepared, you see. They have rented a house and the invitations will soon go out for my ball in May.' She sounded very woebegone at the prospect.

'I thought that is what all girls dreamed of,' he said in rallying tones. 'A ball in your honour, and all the trappings of a London season.'

'Maybe they do, but I'm so bad at it,' she wailed, 'I know Mama wishes me to marry as well as possible, so that I can help my sisters. I feel that every man I meet is looking me over as a prospective bride, and finding me sadly wanting. Mama will be so disappointed.'

'She would not push you into an unhappy alliance?' He was angry at the thought.

'Oh, no, nothing of that kind. But I know she would expect me to do my duty, if it is possible, and choose someone suitable. Only I cannot believe that anyone will offer for me at all. Or if he did, it would be an old man who wishes for a young wife, or a rich Cit wanting to marry into a titled family,' she said baldly.

'You would not accept such a match.'

'Of course I wouldn't want to. But I do want to help Papa, and Mama, and my sisters. I must do my best for the family.'

'I should not permit it,' he said firmly.

She looked at him dubiously. 'You are very good, but what could you do?'

He could think of several things, beginning with a few home truths to Lady Cornelia, who in fact little merited his anger. With Harriet's eyes fixed on his face in surprise he could think of nothing to say, so turned the conversation. 'I cannot understand why you should think that nobody will offer for you. You are not an antidote, you know!'

This poor sally raised a trembling smile, but she shook her head. 'You do not know—you have not seen me. I never know how to talk to people.'

'You talk to me, and I am "people".'

'But you are my friend. When I am at a party, all dressed up, I don't feel like myself. My brain goes numb and all I can do is utter inanities.'

'Then you are like most people, surely?'

'It is the way that I say them. Somehow my voice is all wrong, and in a crowd no one can hear what I am saying. And then I am so clumsy. When I dance I trip over my skirts, and tread on my partner's feet, and I cannot do the Curtsy!'

'You are just too nervous. If you were dancing with someone you knew, and liked, you would be perfectly all right.'

'But I don't know them, or hardly at all,' she pointed out. 'There will be a few of our local friends that I know, I suppose, but we have never been able to afford to spend much time in London. They will all be strangers, and they will think me stupid, and laugh at me.'

Her tone of despair was almost comical, but he saw that her nightmares were as real to her as his were to him, and hid his amusement with very real sympathy. 'And the Curtsy—what is that?'

'I have to do it when I am presented to the Queen. And then I must walk backwards, in a grand dress with enormous skirts, and a train. I shall fall flat.'

'Surely it is only practice?'

'If you knew how I have practiced—for weeks and weeks, with Mama and Amanda. And I have never yet managed to do it properly. I just fall over.'

'Then I can see I shall have to take you in hand. Come, now, that is what friends are for. You have advised me on my farm, and now *I* shall help *you*. You shall be drilled!' Harriet looked dubious, but rose obediently. 'Now what is it you have to do, exactly? We shall break it down move by move, and do it by numbers. Company, on parade!'

Laughing, Harriet stood to attention. There was a small area of relatively smooth grass, and Robert waved her to the far side of it while he himself remained seated on his log. First he made her pace forward slowly, counting aloud to keep the steps even.

'Now, slowly, down ... two ... three ... hold it ... four ... five ... up ... six ... seven ... eight ... no, don't step back yet. Give yourself another count of two to get your balance properly, then right foot ... left ... three ... four ... you see? That wasn't bad. Go through it again.'

They repeated the exercise several times, with Robert counting aloud. At last he stood up. 'That was much better! We'll do it once more.'

'My knees are aching,' protested Harriet.

'Just one more time, and you must count it in your head. I shall be the Queen.'

Carefully Harriet trod across the grass, her lips moving silently. Reaching Robert she sank into a deep reverence, touching the outstretched hand of the supposed monarch. In the act of rising, she looked up, and immediately her composure fled. Robert was looking primly down, his cheeks slightly puffed out and his lips pursed into the familiar tight smile. Harriet gave a gasp of laughter and a wild wobble, clutching desperately at the hand she had been timidly touching as she felt her balance going.

His hand grasped hers in a reassuring grip, and he bent to support her with his free arm, catching her round the waist and lifting her bodily to her feet. She had never been held so closely by a man before, and felt a sense of suffocation, feeling her heart suddenly pounding. Yet the feeling strangely held no fear, and she leaned trustingly into his embrace, her face raised wonderingly to his.

Robert was confused. His experience of women was confined to a few affairs with compliant women of a lower class, when he was younger. He had been very careful, in his dealings with well-born ladies, not to compromise himself by dallying too flirtatiously. Now Harriet's young body was deliciously pliant in his arms, and the scent of the rosebags that clung about her clothes wafted headily about him. Her cheeks were as smooth and soft as petals, and scarcely knowing what he did, he bent further and kissed them. She did not start away, but swayed closer to him, her eyes closing as he kissed her lips, gently at first, then with rising passion as he felt her instant response.

For a long moment they clung together, then he raised his head and slackened the tightened hold of his arms. His voice was husky. 'I'm sorry.' It seemed inadequate. He did not know what to say. She smiled up at him.

'That is not very gallant,' she teased him gently. 'I am not sorry at all.'

'You should be slapping my face, or swooning away,' he said almost roughly. He did not yet understand his own feelings, and was shaken by what had occurred. He was almost affronted by her calmness. Part of him wanted to snatch his arms away from her and make off, never to see her again, and part of him wanted to hold her close, and kiss her again.

'I told you I am not very ladylike,' she said ruefully. 'I have never been kissed before. I suppose Mama would be horrified, but I do not at all want to slap you. I like it. I suppose if I had known it would happen, I would have had to do something to prevent it, but I believe we were both taken by surprise, and I'm glad.'

'Your Mama would indeed be horrified. This is precisely why you should not allow yourself to be alone with a strange man.'

'You are not a strange man. You are my friend, Mr Roberts,' she pointed out. 'Oh, I cannot continue to call you "Mr Roberts". What is your given name?'

'Robert,' he said without thinking.

'"Robert Roberts"—how very... singular.'

She was trying not to laugh, and he had to smile. 'I do not know what the person who named me was thinking of,' he said.

'There, now you are smiling again. Can we not forget that this has happened, if it worries you? I do not want to lose my friend,' she said wistfully.

He took her hand and looked earnestly down at her. 'Does it matter so much, then, our friendship?'

She nodded. 'More than anything.'

He released her hand. 'It is getting late. You should go back. I am sorry I was so abrupt—as you say, I took myself by surprise. You are right, we must not spoil our friendship. It matters a great deal to me, too. We will talk about it tomorrow. We both need time for thought. Now, be off, they will wonder where you have been, it is getting so late.' He did not offer to kiss her again, but she took his hand and raised it for a moment to her cheek. Then she was gone. He watched her run away down the path, with True bounding at her heels. Half unconsciously, he raised the hand she had caressed to his own cheek, and held it there for a moment. He did not stir until the sound of her running feet had vanished into the distance.

THE REST of the afternoon passed by in a daze for Harriet, and she could not afterwards remember it, nor how she had passed the first half of the evening. The rest of the family were cheerful, because Lady Cornelia had announced that she would come downstairs again on the following day. She had been allowed to leave her bed that afternoon, and had suffered no ill effects at all.

'I am so pleased that Mama is better,' said Amanda at dinner. 'The doctor has said there is no longer any fear of infection, so you may visit her later, Harriet. I looked for you during the afternoon, for you could have come up then, but I could not find you. I suppose you were outside.'

'I suppose I was,' replied Harriet vaguely. She hardly heard what her sister was saying. She was naturally glad that her mother was better, but since the illness had not been severe she had been in no apprehension of any danger to her mother, so there was no sudden relief of tension. Her mind was fully taken up with the events of the afternoon, and the rest of her family had as little reality for her as ghosts.

After dinner she visited her mother. Lady Cornelia was lying on a day-bed in her little upstairs sitting room, dressed in a loose afternoon gown. At her daughter's entrance she sat up and spoke with her usual briskness.

'There you are, my dear. I am glad to see you after all this time.'

'And I you, Mama. I am so glad you are better.'

'Thank you, Harriet. I am more than happy to be so, and even happier to find that you have escaped infection. When I think that I scolded you for not accompanying me to Mrs Amberley's—well, I would not wish you to make a habit of such disobedience, but I must own that for this once it was a blessing that you did. Come over here and let me look at you. I hear that you have been spending much of your time outside. Your father says your looks are much improved. Yes, a little tanned, perhaps, but your colour is good.' Harriet was blushing slightly at the reference to her walks. 'Naughty girl, you should have been practising your deportment. However, the weather has been very fine, I hear, and I cannot blame you for wishing to enjoy it. Yes, I believe your complexion has improved, for though you always had a good skin you were sometimes very pale.' Harriet's eyes dropped before her mother's scrutiny. 'What is this? Harriet, I do believe there are a few freckles on your nose! You have been allowing the sunlight to fall on your face, and I have told you so often that nothing is so injurious to the skin, even at this time of year.'

'I am sorry, Mama,' murmured Harriet contritely.

'You must put lemon juice on them, night and morning.'

'Yes, Mama.' Harriet sounded so subdued that her mother relented.

'There, my dear, it is of no consequence, they will soon be gone. It is only that I want you to be looking your best, for now that I am recovered we must waste no time. I plan to leave for London in a very few days.'

Harriet was horrified. 'A few days! But Mama...so soon?'

'Now do not give me those die-away airs, Harriet. You know very well that but for my indisposition we should already have been in London. There will be a million and one things to be done before your ball. We have already missed several parties, and I want to take you out as much as possible when we arrive. It is so important that you meet plenty of the right sort of people.'

Harriet thought sadly that the right sort of people might not be very interested in meeting her.

'We shall spend the whole of tomorrow going through your clothes,' decided Lady Cornelia. 'I wish to see that all is just as it should be before they are packed. Now, what is the matter, Harriet?'

'Nothing, Mama,' said Harriet, trying to control her trembling lips. 'I have the headache, a little.'

Lady Cornelia sat up once again to feel her forehead. 'Do not tell me that you are sickening for something, after all this time! You feel cool enough, at all events. Have you any other pain?'

'Oh, no, I am very well. Perhaps I am a little tired from—from my walk. And the sun was very bright.' In her eagerness to reassure her mother Harriet realised that she had all but put it out of her power to go out of doors on the following day, and she started to gabble about fresh air.

'Then you had better be off to bed at once,' her mother cut her short. 'We have a busy day ahead of us, and I shall expect to see you bright and early tomorrow.'

Harriet lay quietly in the bed she still shared with Amanda, staring with unseeing eyes at the familiar pattern of moonlight shining through chinks in the curtain on the tester above. Amanda slept peacefully at her side. Harriet had dawdled over her preparations for bed, brushing and braiding her hair very slowly, and anointing the freckles several times with anxious care, so that by the time she was ready Amanda was almost asleep, and disinclined for the usual bedtime conversation.

Harriet's mind was full of questions. Inexperienced though she was in love, she knew that for her no other man could now take any place in her heart. With that kiss he had taken possession of her, and she regarded herself as his alone. About Robert's feelings she was not so sure. When she thought of the strength of his arms around her, and the ardour of his kisses, a thrill of something that was almost pain shot through her body. At those moments she was sure that she was loved. But she knew from her brother Harry's conversation, in moments of careless confidence, that many men loved easily, even lightly, and that such feelings did not necessarily last. If he loved her, she would be happy to brave the displeasure of family and friends for the sake of being with him. He was not, after all, a pauper, and he was a gentleman. She was not so romantic as to believe in a 'happy ever after' world of love in a cottage. She would have to work, to learn to do things she had never done before, but though she was an Earl's daughter she felt well enough fitted to be a farmer's wife.

In the end, her only comfort was that he was her friend. He had said so himself. Her love and loyalty were given now to him, but if he demanded no more of her than her continuing friendship, she told herself that she must learn to make that enough. She could not think of marriage to any other, but somehow she must persuade her parents to let her stay at home, so that Amanda could have her chance of making the good marriage that had passed her sister by. In her present exalted mood, even that seemed a good and hopeful thing. Comforted, she turned on her side and went to sleep.

ROBERT, TOO, LAY awake. He wondered what he had done, and could almost have cursed himself for that moment's weakness. The last thing he had intended to do at this time was to fall in love, especially with a girl such as Harriet, for whom the only possible outcome of such a love would be marriage. And yet...

He thought of her as he had first seen her. No beauty, certainly, but he had long ceased to notice that. Her eyes were lovely, and her smile. He liked the way her head was poised on her slender neck by her heavy coils of hair, that would keep slipping down no matter what she did. He liked the way her thoughts could so easily be read in her face. She was honest, and open, and brave too. Was this not exactly what he had looked for in a wife? A woman who could be a companion and friend, as well as a lover. Then he thought of her going to London, dancing in other men's arms, perhaps even being proposed to by them, and at once a pang of fierce jealously shot through him. He smiled to himself. It was as simple as that, then. He loved her, and he thought she loved him. He would see her tomorrow, and ask her. Still smiling, he too, fell asleep.

He was no longer smiling the next day, however, as he waited by the hammerpond in the woods. For half an hour he had stood there, keyed up with excitement, and she had not come. He kicked the log, frowning down at it. Had he, after all frightened her the day before? Had she had second thoughts after she had left him? She most know that in his present character he was far beneath her. A Mr Roberts of nowhere in particular does not aspire to the hand of an Earl's daughter. Nor is that Earl likely to welcome such a match.

He had just decided that she would not be coming when he heard her hurried approach. She ran through the trees, breathless and flustered, and at once such thoughts vanished. He opened his arms and she flew into them like a bird to its nest, lifting her face to his kiss with the child-like candour he loved.

'I am sorry I am so late. Did you think I was not coming?'

'I had begun to wonder. After yesterday...'

'After yesterday, how could I not come? The trouble is, Mama is better.'

She spoke in tones of doom, and he had to laugh. 'Unnatural girl! You would surely not wish her to be worse!'

That brought a smile, as he had thought it would.

'No, of course not. What I mean is that she is up, and downstairs. She has kept me with her all day, trying on my new gowns. Only, thank goodness, Amanda thought she should rest this afternoon, as it is her first day out of her room. She persuaded Mama to lie down for a while, so I was able to slip away. But only for a little time, for I must be there when she comes down again. Oh, Robert, we shall be going to London almost immediately. It is so dreadful!'

'No, no,' he soothed. 'You will enjoy yourself.'

'How can I, when I must leave you here?'

'Don't worry about that. I shall come to London too.' She still looked uncertain. He took her hand and kissed it. 'Harriet, my dearest, I must call on your Papa.'

She smiled tremulously. 'You mean...?'

'To ask him for your hand. May I do that, Harriet?'

'Oh yes, but...' she paused, not knowing how to continue.

'I have not mistaken your feelings in this matter?'

She gave him one of the direct looks he loved. 'No, Robert. I love you with all my heart, and I will be proud to be your wife. Even if that is not to be, I shall always regard myself as yours. Only I am afraid Papa and Mama

may not like it, just at first. You will not be hurt, will you,
by anything they may say?'

'I promise I shall not,' he answered tenderly, knowing
that as the rich Sir Robert Atherington they were likely to
welcome him into the family with open arms. 'But you . . .
Will they not be angry with you?'

'Yes, I suppose they will. But I shall not mind that, if
you do not. We may have to wait for a while, of course.
But I know they do truly desire my happiness, and when
they see that we are in earnest, they must agree in the end.
At least, I hope so.'

'And you would submit to all this, for me?' he asked,
much struck.

'Of course. How can you doubt it?'

'Bravest of girls.' He tightened his hold and kissed her
again, feeling her body quiver in response to his eager
kisses. After a few moments she struggled from his hold.

'I must go back, Robert. Already Mama might be wondering where I am.'

'Harriet! Wait! There is something I must tell you!'

Already she was among the trees. His pleasure had been
so great, in finding that Harriet was prepared to love him
as mere Mr Roberts, that he had postponed his explanation too long. His chance was gone. Her voice floated back
to him. 'Tell me in London, Robert. I shall see you there.'

Robert sighed, and began to walk back to the farm,
wondering how he was to explain to the Johnsons that he
must leave at once. He would return to Atherington to pick
up Barton, and his London clothes. He could not call on
the Earl dressed like this.

Lady Cornelia was pleased to see that Harriet had recovered her usual sunny disposition in the afternoon. In
the morning she had seemed distracted, uninterested in the

bustle of preparations. Now she was all compliance and smiles.

'Really, Harriet, you look positively beautiful in that pink and white ball-gown. I think you should wear that one for our own ball. The apple-blossom should be out by then; I shall have some sent up from here, and we shall use it to catch up the flounces. I believe it would suit your style very well. In fact—my dear, I have had an idea, and I think it might just be the thing I have been looking for, to make our ball a little different from all the others. What do you say to decorating the house entirely with country flowers?'

'The very thing, Mama!' exclaimed Amanda. 'As you say, it will suit our dear Harriet so well, and think how pretty! Only, they will not last well, so they must be done at the last moment. Still, that can be managed, can it not, Mama?'

To Harriet the idea seemed to crown the happiness of the day. To dance with Robert in a sea of apple-blossom exactly suited her ideas.

'Thank you, Mama, it would be wonderful! I should like it of all things.'

'Then that is settled. I shall speak to the gardener presently. Now let me see your curtsy, Harriet. I hope you have been practising?'

'Oh, yes.' And, to her mother's astonishment, and watched by an open-mouthed Amanda, Harriet floated across the room, sank gracefully into a deep curtsy, and rose without a wobble. Lady Cornelia could have wept.

'Harriet, my dear girl, I should never have doubted you!'

'Thank you, Mama,' repeated Harriet demurely.

CHAPTER EIGHT

IF THE JOHNSONS were surprised to hear of Robert's abrupt departure, they did not show it. However discreet Robert might have thought he had been, his afternoon absences had not gone unnoticed. The countryside is seldom as empty as it looks, and local people had an eye to what their young lady was doing. One word from the gamekeeper, her brother, was enough for Mrs Johnson, though she had cautioned him to tell no one else, and to keep his eyes open that nothing untoward happened to Lady Harriet.

'He's a good worker, when he's here, for all his gentlemanly ways,' admitted her husband. 'But some days he'll take himself off in the afternoon, and be gone for more than an hour. I don't mind, I'm not paying him, after all. But what's he really up to?'

Mrs Johnson had taken steps of her own. As the wife of the Earl's tenant, she could not allow any harm to come to Lady Harriet, however romantic it might be. A stern letter to her cousin had elicited a reluctant response, while swearing her to secrecy.

'He's up to no harm, I'll be bound,' she said comfortably. 'You know he's had a bad time out there fighting those nasty Russians. He did say he needed some peace.'

Johnson grunted. They had both been woken more than once by Robert's shouts when in the grip of a nightmare, and he had apologised in a shame-faced fashion on his first arriving. Mrs Johnson had noticed that such incidents had ceased during the last week, and drew her own conclusions. A healthy body, and a mind more at peace with itself, was her diagnosis. She would have agreed well with Lady Beatrice. She also had a pretty good idea of which way the wind was blowing with Robert and Harriet, and her motherly heart rejoiced to see it. As a struggling young farmer he could only barely be considered a match for the Earl's eldest daughter, but as a wealthy baronet he was what the vulgar world would call 'a good catch' for a girl of no more than moderate beauty, and less fortune. So she held her tongue, and distracted her husband as far as possible from Robert's frequent absences during the afternoon. Thus his decision to leave came as no surprise, as the country grapevine had already reported Lady Cornelia's recovery, and surmised the family's imminent removal to London. Robert made his farewells with gratitude.

'I have learned much from you, even in these few weeks,' he said to the farmer. 'I hope I may be able to return some day, or at least to send for your advice occasionally. I have at least seen the good results of the methods you use, and hope to try them to advantage myself.'

Johnson, a man of few words, contented himself with a handshake and a gruff promise of help in the future, if needed. Mrs Johnson, to his surprise, dropped him a respectful curtsy, then whisked out a handkerchief to brush a sentimental tear from her eyes.

'I do wish you all happiness, sir,' she said earnestly.

He cast her a searching glance, which she met guilelessly, then delighted her by bending to kiss her cheek.

'Mark my words, Johnson,' she said as she watched her visitor ride away, 'we shall hear of Mr Roberts again. And it will be good news, I hope and trust.'

Her incurious spouse grunted, and left her to her imaginings.

THE WORK on the house was well advanced when Robert reached Atherington Hall. Barton showed him with pride the new bathroom, conveniently close to his bed-chamber. The furniture shone, the windows gleamed, even the roof no longer leaked and a start had been made on replacing the plaster damaged by earlier rainfall.

'With the weather turning so fine, we have gone on with the roof, and I have set some of the men to work in the gardens, Captain,' he said, leading Robert to the window. The straggling old grass of the lawns had been scythed short, and the new growth showed a fresh green. A few neglected old rose bushes had been re-discovered, and old beds dug over and cleared. It was tidy, if a little bare.

'Barton, you have done wonders,' said Robert. The man looked at his master. He thought, but did not say, that the greatest wonder was the change in him. Who would have believed that a few short weeks on a farm could have had such a profound effect. Unless . . . ?

'Barton, we are to go to London.'

So that was it, Barton thought. A woman in the case, and Atherington Hall was to have a mistress, no doubt. He composed his face to a suitably blank expression. 'Very good, Captain. When do you wish to leave?'

'As soon as possible, Barton. It is time I made my bow to polite society. And I must visit my tailor without delay. My evening clothes are in a sad state, as I recall.'

Definitely a woman, thought Barton.

'And you may take that smug look off your face, Barton,' said his master with mock anger. They exchanged a glance of complete understanding and Barton felt his spirits lift. Here was the Captain back, the Captain as he had been before the war. Who ever this woman was, what ever she was like, Barton swore at that moment to serve her with devotion and gratitude. Whistling, he went to see to the packing.

A busy day was given over to estate affairs, and two more days brought them to London. Robert at once sallied forth to his tailor's, there to gladden that worthy gentleman's heart by the number of garments he wished to order. Barton went to inspect a short list of lodgings suitable for a single gentleman of ample means.

Further reflection had made Robert realise that to call without warning on the Earl and demand to marry Harriet might lead to an unpleasant degree of surprise, and some discomfort for his betrothed. He was in no doubt that his suit would be received with complaisance, but was reluctant to admit that they had been meeting clandestinely in the country. Not for anything would he expose her to her parents' displeasure, or the gossip of the world. They must meet, he decided, as if for the first time, in London. An instant attraction, a lightning romance, and the world would be satisfied.

It had seemed so easy while he was planning it, but it was not until he came to put it into effect that he realised the problems involved. He was, to all intents and purposes, completely unacquainted with Harriet's family. After his absence in the Crimea he had few acquaintances in London, and these dated mostly from his younger days. He had lost so many of his army friends during the war, and since his return had deliberately withdrawn from any contact with his former friends. Now he cursed himself for his lack of foresight. He was singularly unencumbered with relatives. An only child himself, his late parents had themselves been only children. The one relative with whom he was at all close was Lady Beatrice, and she was in Bath, where she had lived for many years.

On his return from the wars he had spent as little time as possible in London, and had shunned his former acquaintance, refusing the small number of invitations that came his way. As a result, the few people he knew were unlikely to invite him again. For a mad moment he considered loitering outside the house in Grosvenor Square that the Earl had taken for the season. Further reflection showed him that even if he caught sight of Harriet, it would not be likely to lead to a meeting.

In desperation he wrote to his aunt, begging for her help in the matter, or at least her advice. Knowing that her robust sense of humour would overcome any worries about the propriety of his behaviour, he told her the whole story, ending with a eulogy on his beloved's charms, and begging for help.

His trust was not misplaced. Lady Beatrice laughed heartily over the charade, shook her head over the meetings and sighed with impatience over his failure to confess to his beloved what he had done. Wiser than he in the ways of young girls in the throes of their first love, she foresaw tempests on the horizon, particularly if the girl was as headstrong as, from her behaviour and her mother's report, she appeared to be.

Needless to say, a large part of her amusement derived from the fact that he had unwittingly fallen in love with the one girl she had already picked out for him. Not for worlds would she have him know, at this juncture, that she had already written to the Countess about him, for she knew well that any overt attempt to push him into Harriet's arms would be likely to have the reverse effect. She took pity on his desperation, however, and replied at once. After taking him to task for his ill-considered behaviour, she continued:

> ... but I shall say no more on that subject, for I am sure you know very well how wrongly you have behaved. I only hope the Young Lady will be as understanding as I, but since she obviously loves you *'à folie'*, no doubt she will forgive.
>
> As to your other difficulties, I am happy to be able to say that I am in a position to help. I was very well acquainted with Lady Cornelia's mother, and in fact stood god-mother to her (Lady Cornelia, that is). I have not seen her for many years, in fact not since I came to live in Bath. After my friend Edwina Dulverton died I kept up a correspondence with my god-daughter. I shall write to her mentioning your name, and I think you may be justified in calling on them.
>
> I can only say, my dear great-nephew, that I am glad to find that my assessment of your needs was so accurate. Bring your Harriet to see me, when you are wed. I shall be glad to make her acquaintance. I remain, dear boy, your affect. Great Aunt,
>
> > Beatrice Fitzpaine.

Robert was delighted. Scarcely pausing to finish reading the letter he snatched his hat and gloves, and took himself off to Grosvenor Square, not pausing to think, in his excitement, that he was scarcely on such terms as to call at the house in the morning hours. His heart pounding, he trod up the imposing steps and was admitted by the butler. A disappointment, however, awaited him. The Earl, he was told upon enquiry, was not at home.

'If I might pay my respects to the Countess?' Robert continued, in what he was surprised to find was a calm voice.

'I regret, sir, that her ladyship is also out.'

Robert looked at him blankly. 'Out? Do you expect her to return soon?'

'I should not like to say, sir. Her ladyship has gone out with the young ladies. I believe an expedition to the shops was mentioned.'

'I see,' Robert stared dumbly at him. It had simply not occurred to him that they would not be there.

The butler took pity on him. 'If you would like to leave your card, sir?'

'My card? Oh, yes, of course.' Robert fished feverishly in his pockets and handed his card to the butler, who received it impassively. A wild plan of enlisting the butler's help in contacting Harriet herself died an early death as he looked at the noble countenance that stared benignly at a point somewhere over his left shoulder. In fact he wronged the good man, who was devoted to Harriet, having been with the family since she was a small child, and who would happily have compromised his position by accepting any number of illicit notes for his young mistress, even without suitable remuneration.

This, however, Robert was not to know. Gathering what dignity he could, he turned and left the house. He spent the rest of the day haunting the fashionable shops, scanning the crowds for Harriet. He was out of luck.

Lady Cornelia, determined to give her eldest daughter the best appearance she could, was forced by circumstances to study economy. Not for her the fashionable—and very expensive—shops where Robert loitered so hopefully. Cousin Alice, who had been so helpful in the matter of the new crinoline, had told her of some really useful places, quite out of the way, where one could purchase such important items as gloves and stockings, of good quality, and at half the price. Lady Cornelia, Harriet and Amanda had spent an enthralling morning, and returned home laden with a small mountain of parcels.

Harriet, hurrying upstairs with her sister to enjoy a leisurely unpacking and examination of their booty, paused hopefully when she heard the butler say that a gentleman had called. For a moment she held her breath. Lady Cornelia examined the card.

'Sir Robert Atherington. I don't believe... Oh yes, I remember. A relation of my god-mother. How very civil of him to call so soon, I received a letter from her only this morning, saying that he was in town. I must be sure to send him a card to your ball, Harriet.'

Disappointed, Harriet continued up the stairs. Disappointment, however, could not long contend with the delights of six pairs of fine silk stockings, kid gloves of every conceivable shade, and a really very fashionable bonnet, that needed only a slight alteration to its trimming by Amanda's clever fingers to make it look quite Bond Street.

UNDAUNTED by his failure, Robert sallied forth in the evening to the opera. It is to be regretted that he heard none of the music, for he spent the first half of the performance scanning the boxes to see if Harriet were present. She was not, so during the interval he left Covent Garden and made his way to the theatre. Another search proved equally fruitless. The Milbornes had, in fact, gone to a small private party given by a friend of Lady Cornelia, and Harriet had spent an uncomfortable few hours listening to a very boring young man who had pronounced views on the late war. Harriet put up with him for as long as she could, but since she knew from talking to

Robert that he was quite ill-informed, she eventually silenced him with one short, decisive speech that left him with his mouth hanging open.

'For all the world like a cod's head,' giggled Harriet to Amanda in the privacy of their bedchamber.

'Was Mama very cross?'

'I'm afraid she was. It seems he is a very wealthy young man.' Harriet did not sound very repentant.

Robert ended his disappointing day by getting quietly drunk at his club with two army friends he encountered there. They grew mildly hilarious, and he walked home feeling happier than he had expected after such a day.

The following morning saw him morosely nursing an aching head at the breakfast table. Barton entered with the post. Two bills, a letter from an old schoolfriend who had heard of his return, and something else. Without much interest he slit the envelope and pulled out the card.

Lady Cornelia had acted with her usual prompt efficiency. Informed by her god-mother that Robert was in town, and was actively interested in finding himself a wife, she had acted on the hint. A smile spread over his face as he looked down at the contents of the final envelope. It was an invitation to Harriet's ball.

CHAPTER NINE

FOR A FEW days after their arrival in Grosvenor Square, Harriet was in such a whirl that she scarcely had time to draw breath, and at night she sank almost at once into an exhausted slumber. Although used to leading an active life, she found the constant noise and bustle exhausting. Her feet ached from hard pavements, and her back from sitting demurely on uncomfortable little chairs paying an endless round of calls with her mother.

Having lost some valuable time, Lady Cornelia was determined not to waste a moment more. First, and most important, a visit to the modiste for a fitting of that vital creation, the Presentation Dress. Then visits, parties, the theatre, the opera—all the haunts of fashionable life. Harriet met so many new people that she found herself unable to recall the names of any of them. Her cheeks aching from smiling, she comforted herself that it was not for long. Soon Robert would come, and all of this would be a thing of the past. Nevertheless, for the sake of Mama who had put so much effort into her coming out, she must continue to smile, and agree, and sit without fidgeting.

After about a week, she found herself more accustomed. No longer did she wake six times a night and lie listening to the sounds from the square outside. She started to recognise faces and to recall names. Her patent lack of interest in the young men she met did her no disservice: she was pronounced a very modest, prettily-behaved girl by her elders. Other young ladies found her delightful, seeing that she presented little competition to their charms, and most men found her relaxing, if abstracted, company. Her own inner happiness cast a glow of joy over her face, and made it easy for her to remain cheerful even when she was tired.

After a week, however, there was a slight change. As the days went by without a sight of Robert, she started to wonder—not whether he was unfaithful, but whether he was unwell, or perhaps just fearful of the snubbing set-down she had predicted. Her glowing looks dimmed day by day, her complexion lost its colour, she seemed to her anxious mother to be losing her first attraction.

Amanda, closer in age and affection to Harriet, noted that her sister started when there was a knock at the front door, and that Harriet would look hopefully as the butler admitted a visitor, only to subside in dejection when she saw who it was. She also noticed that whenever possible Harriet stationed herself close to the window, where she could see out into the street. Her own delicate sense of honour forbade her to question her sister on a subject on which she appeared unwilling to speak, but she knew that Harriet often slept restlessly, and awoke in the morning unrefreshed.

April turned into May, and the day of the ball grew ever closer. Lady Cornelia was engrossed in consultations with caterers, musicians and decorators. She had wisely kept to her decision that the opulent hot-house flowers generally used on such occasions were not suited to Harriet's kind of beauty. Instead there were flowers from the countryside. Lady Cornelia preened herself that it would be quite out of the way, an original idea that would make her ball the talk of the town. From the estate were to come baskets of blossom—apple, wild cherry, bunches of wild hyacinths and even, greatly daring since it was really a weed, sprays of delicate Queen Anne's Lace.

'Don't know why you want to deck the place out with weeds, my dear,' said the Earl morosely. 'I spend most of my life trying to get rid of them. And picking apple-blossom! We shan't have an apple to our name this autumn, you mark my words.'

'Nonsense,' retorted his wife briskly. 'You know very well I have said they must take as much as possible from the wild crab-apples. And think of all the money it will save! It would cost a small fortune to deck the ballroom with bought hot-house blooms.'

The Earl had to agree that there was something in this, but added a further word of warning. 'Mustn't look penny-pinching, though, my dear. Don't want people saying we can't afford to do things properly.'

'I do not think there is any risk of that, Henry. I have hired the best orchestra, and the food for the supper is of the highest quality. No, I hope to achieve a charming and original effect, and no one is going to talk of penny-pinching after they have had a glass of the pink champagne you ordered. That was inspired, my dear. It gives just the touch I wanted.'

'Just as you say, my lady. I'm sure you know what you're doing. You usually do. I just hope those precious weeds of yours do not wilt before anyone has had the chance of seeing them.'

'It is a problem, I know. They cannot be done until the very last moment. However, the ballroom is cool, and as long as they last for the first hour or two I shall be satisfied. Are you sure you have ordered sufficient champagne? It would not do to run out.'

'Enough to float a battleship,' groaned the Earl, taking himself hastily off to the comparative peace of his library, where he buried himself in a monograph on sheep and tried not to remember that this would all be to do again for Amanda, not to mention all the other girls. It made him shudder. He hated being in London.

Through the bustle of preparations Harriet moved with increasing gloom. On the afternoon of the day itself she drifted round the house, unable to rest although she knew she should be building up her energies for the night to come.

Even in her abstraction, she had to admit that the house looked beautiful. In the ballroom and the principal saloons great branches of blossom grew like small trees, their bases masked with drifts of bluebells and Queen Anne's Lace. There were none of the huge, formal arrangements of flowers usual to such occasions. Instead, smaller posies of the same flowers were on every available surface, and the supper tables were festooned with garlands of fresh green leaves, studded with knots of blossom. The effect was of some pastoral fete, a delightful mixture of the simple and the sophisticated.

'If only Robert were here to see it,' thought Harriet, 'how happy I should be.'

Her thoughts were interrupted by a bustle in the hall, and the sound of a familiar voice speaking to the butler.

'Harry!' shrieked Harriet, running to the source of the noise, and flinging her arms round the tall, smartly dressed young man who was in the act of removing his gloves. 'Oh, Harry, how *very* good of you to come! I had thought you were not going to be here for my ball, and I was so sorry. How did you get leave?'

'Oh, well, eldest sister, first ball, you know,' murmured her brother, gently disengaging her stranglehold round his neck, and smoothing the set of his coat lovingly, casting an anxious glance in the looking glass as he did so. 'Steady on, old girl, there's no need to throttle me!' he added, tempering the words with a hug and kiss, for the two of them were close in age and had always been good friends.

'I thought you didn't really want to come?'

'Oh, well, balls, you know, not really my line of business. Not really yours either, I'd have thought, but I suppose you haven't any choice. Still, I wanted to make a dash to London, see about a bit of business, so I thought, why not?'

'Harry, you wretch, you just made it an excuse to get leave of absence,' she accused, laughing. He laughed back sheepishly, but she thought she detected a look of strain under the smile.

'Are you in some kind of trouble, dearest?' she asked lovingly. He began to bluster a denial, but she was not taken in. She knew him too well, and was worried to see an almost desperate look in his eyes. 'You must tell me! I shall help,' she said.

'You can't. No one can,' he almost groaned, but at that moment they were interrupted.

'St Erth! My dear boy, what a delightful surprise.' Lady Cornelia, warned by the butler, was making her stately way downstairs. 'Harriet, my dear, you should be very much obliged to your brother, and I know you are glad to see him, but you should be resting on your bed. St Erth, your father is in the library. I am rather occupied just now, but I shall look forward to a long chat with you later. How long can you stay?'

'Not long, ma'am, only a day or two,' he said, dutifully kissing her proffered cheek.

Harriet clutched his arm. 'Come and see me as soon as you have finished with Papa,' she hissed. Her brother nodded and went.

He found her later reclining on a sofa in her dressing room. Amanda was luckily helping the Countess, so they were able to be alone. When he came in she swung her legs down to the floor, and patted the place beside her invitingly.

'There, now, sit down and tell me all about it. Is it money? Are you in debt again? I am afraid I have been shockingly spendthrift since we came to London, but I still have a bit of my allowance left, if you need it.'

He took her hand gratefully. 'No, it's not that, at least not exactly. Papa was very good at Christmas, and helped me out with some debts. I promised him I wouldn't let them get so bad again, and I stuck to it.'

'Then what is it?'

He looked uncomfortable. 'The thing is, Hetty, it's not the sort of thing a fellow can really talk about—at least, not to his sister. Not suitable, you know.' The use of his childhood nickname for her showed her how worried he really was.

'Then it is a female, I suppose,' she said composedly.

'How did you know?'

She laughed at his air of a naughty boy caught out. 'Goodness, Harry, I am not that much of an innocent! Who is she?'

'She works in a shop. In Oxford. She is so pretty, Hetty, you wouldn't believe! I know everyone says Amanda is a beauty, but Annie...golden curls, and such eyes! Her figure, too, so graceful, and the loveliest laugh you ever heard.'

'So, you fell in love with her?'

'Yes. Oh, it was all very innocent, Harriet, or I should not be telling you of it,' he added, sounding more boyish than ever. 'We went for walks together, and once or twice I had tea at her house.'

'Is that why you didn't come home at Easter?'

'Yes, I couldn't bear to leave her.'

'Oh, Harry, I do understand how you feel, truly I do.'

Her brother, sunk in his own worries, scarcely noticed the fervour of her words. 'Well, thank you, Hetty. But that's not all. I wrote her some poems.'

'Some poems?' she echoed blankly, struggling with this new image of her brother. How clearly she remembered, but a few months before, hearing him say that all poetry was half-baked, soft stuff, when he had heard her admiring the work of Tennyson.

'Yes, some poems,' he repeated impatiently. 'All about how I loved her, and wanted to make her mine... You know the sort of stuff.'

'How—how delightful,' she hazarded.

'And I gave them to her,' he continued gloomily. 'And now her father says she is expecting to marry me. He says it is in the poems.'

'And is it?'

'No! Yes! I suppose so,' he finished lamely. 'I can't really remember what I did say, to tell the truth. And I don't know what to do, for her father says if I don't marry her it will be breach of contract, or something, and I shall have to go to court. Oh, Hetty, what will Papa say, when he has been so good to me? What shall I do?'

He was in despair, and did not really expect any helpful answer from his sister. He wanted, though, her sympathy in this awful fix, and perhaps her promise of support. Her answer was not at all what he anticipated.

'Do!' cried Harriet in ringing tones. 'Do! Why, you must marry her, of course!'

'Marry her! But she's not... We...not of our class, Harriet. I mean, she's a lovely girl, and good and all that, but she works in a shop, and dash it all, Harriet, I'll be the Earl of Pontesford, some day.'

His sister looked at him with scorn. 'You didn't mind about that when you were writing your poems, and telling her that you loved her. Poor girl! How can you be so cruel? She must be breaking her heart.'

Harry was fairly sure that the lovely Annie was doing no such thing, but he was given no chance to say so. Harriet, her own heart aching because she had offered to give up everything for her love, and had apparently been forgotten, put herself in Annie's place and rounded on him with scorn. 'You must marry her, Harry. No gentleman would do less. How can you think of casting her aside, and saying she is not good enough?'

'It isn't like that,' he protested. 'I never asked her to marry me. It was just a bit of fun, that's all.'

'For you, maybe, but not for that poor girl, with her prospects blighted and her heart given to you. I, for one, will welcome her into the family. Oh, you could not be so cruel as to abandon her!'

Feeling that he had somehow strayed into a melodrama, Harry sat stunned. Unaware of his sister's state of heart, he thought she must have run mad. He decided he must humour her. Obviously the excitement of coming to London, and having her own ball, was too much for her.

'Very well, Hetty, only don't cry now, there's a good girl. You mustn't make your eyes red. Good heavens, look at the time! You should be starting to get ready. This is your evening, you know.'

'I don't really care for it,' she sniffed. 'I'm sorry I said all those things, Harry, and of course you did not mean to be unkind. But if this poor girl loves you, and thinks that you love her...'

'Yes, well,' he said uncomfortably. 'We'll talk about it later. Tomorrow. Now wash your face and I'll be off.'

Listlessly, Harriet did as he said. Her maid arrived, full of excitement. Harriet submitted dumbly to her ministrations, but she found it hard to show any enthusiasm.

CHAPTER TEN

LADY CORNELIA cast a glance of deep satisfaction round the ballroom. Her success, she felt, was assured. Her floral decorations had succeeded beyond her greatest hopes, and had been much admired by a certain Royal Personage who had put in a brief, but very acceptable, appearance. As for Harriet—Lady Cornelia glanced anxiously round the room, and saw her daughter dancing with St Erth. She frowned slightly; she should not be wasting a dance on a mere brother. However, there were plenty more dances yet, and she had to admit that they made an attractive couple. For a moment her mind leapt ahead. Once Harriet was safely off her hands, what could she not do with Amanda? She had been half tempted to let the younger girl come down and join the ball, at least for the earlier half of the evening, but had wisely decided not to allow Amanda to outshine Harriet, even simply dressed as she would have been.

Not that Harriet was looking anything but pretty. Lady Cornelia had expended her considerable taste lavishly, and the result, even to her critical eyes, was excellent. Of deceptively simple cut, the almost transparent white silk tarlatan overskirt floated in tiers above an underskirt of delicate pink silk. The tarlatan was caught up with little knots of fresh apple-blossom, and more of the pink and white flowers were set in Harriet's hair. The effect was enchanting. Beneath the tightly corseted waist, (no nonsense about loose stay laces tonight), the wide bell of pink and white frothed out, swaying with the graceful movement of the new hoops beneath, like the petals of another apple-blossom, miraculously magnified.

Even Harriet had to admit that she was enjoying herself. She had stood with Papa and Mama to receive the guests, and had been both surprised and pleased at the admiring glances she had seen directed towards her. It was heady stuff for a girl who had been used to regard herself as plain and dull. There was no sign of Robert, but she hardly expected to see him, for how could he have had a card? Even so, now that she was released from her duty, her status as daughter of the house meant that she had no lack of partners.

She enjoyed dancing with Harry, for she was still not as proficient in the art as Mama would have liked, and with him she did not need to worry if she accidentally trod on his foot. She had been watching him surreptitiously all evening. He appeared cheerful, but to her loving eye his laughter had a forced, unnatural ring about it, and she was sure he had been drinking more of the pink champagne than was good for him.

'Are you feeling quite well, Harry?' she asked as he took out his handkerchief to wipe his face.

'Just a bit warm, my dear,' he replied firmly. 'All this dancing, you know. Not used to it.'

'I believe you have been drinking too much champagne, Harry,' she said severely.

'Not at all,' he protested in injured tones. 'Dash it all, if a fellow can't have a few glasses of champagne at his sister's come-out ball... There, now, there's this dance coming to an end. Shall I fetch you an ice?'

Before she could dissent, he was gone. She would have followed him, but she was well aware that to argue with him in public would be not at all the thing. She could only hope that the butler, in whose judgment she had every faith, would keep a fatherly eye on him.

The orchestra was striking up again, and she saw her next partner approaching her purposefully. He was rather young man, very self-conscious of his finery, and hiding his bashfulness under a manner which he fondly hoped was man of the world. He bowed. 'Lady Harriet! I believe this dance is mine...' Then his eyes looked beyond her to someone standing just behind, who was actually in the act of putting his hand on her waist.

'On the contrary,' said a deep, familiar voice that shot through her like a streak of lightning, 'I think you will find that Lady Harriet promised this dance to me.'

Harriet whirled round. 'Robert! Oh, Robert!' she gasped.

He smiled down at her. For that moment their eyes met, and they could have been alone once again in their secluded woodland glade.

Harriet's erstwhile partner recalled them. 'Lady Harriet...if you please...the dance...'

Harriet turned a flustered face toward him. 'Oh, I beg your pardon, I am afraid I have made some stupid mistake. I am indeed promised to this gentleman,' she gave a tiny smile at the turn of phrase. 'Please forgive me, Mr...er...' Her voice tailed off, and the young gentleman drew himself up to his not very considerable height.

'Since it seems that you have forgotten not only our dance, but my name, I can only withdraw what must be my unwelcome presence,' he said in tones that he hoped were dignified but which were in fact sadly pompous. He gave a stiff little bow and stalked off, leaving Harriet torn between dismay and laughter.

'Oh, dear, poor young man! I am afraid I have quite forgotten his name. There are so many new people to remember. And then to see you, so suddenly...'

'He'll get over it,' said Robert callously, taking her hand and leading her into the dance. 'We are attracting attention—let us dance.'

Lady Cornelia, searching the room once more for her daughter, was startled. She was dancing with a man who had just apologised to her for arriving late. A relative of her god-mother, Sir Robert something. Perfectly suitable—in fact a good catch, if what Lady Beatrice wrote was true. But she was amazed at her daughter's transformation. The expression of strained seriousness that she habitually wore when concentrating on dancing was gone. Instead she was glowing with happiness, her eyes shining and her cheeks delicately flushed with pink. She seemed to float across the floor, neither tripping nor stumbling in her usual clumsy fashion. It was all very unexpected.

The Earl followed the direction of her gaze. 'Dashed if I've ever seen her look so pretty—a regular beauty tonight. Congratulations, my dear.'

'Congratulations, I think, might be in order, but not to me,' retorted his wife drily.

'Whatever do you mean? That young man? But they've only just met. Never seen him before in my life. Not but what he's a good, upstanding sort of feller. Have a good seat on a horse, I dare say.'

Lady Cornelia gave a ladylike snort. 'A good seat on a horse! What can that signify, pray?'

'To you, not a lot, perhaps. But to Harriet more than a little, I think,' he replied shrewdly, and for once had the satisfaction of silencing her.

Harriet, blissfully circling the ballroom in Robert's arms, had recovered from her first amazement and was eagerly questioning him. 'When did you come to London, Robert? And how did you get in here? I never expected to find you at my ball.'

'I have been in London for some days. Indeed, I called to see you the other day, but you were all out. The trouble was, since I am not supposed to know you, I didn't know how to make your acquaintance, I have been haunting the theatres and the opera in hopes of finding you!'

'Oh, how unlucky, for I never saw you! I was—not worried, precisely, but a little sad that I had not seen you,' she admitted. He held her at a decorous distance, and managed to refrain from tightening his grasp into an embrace, but he squeezed the hand he held.

'I did not wish it to be too apparent that we were already acquainted. I thought it better that we should appear to meet in London. Once I had managed to get hold of an invitation for this ball, I did not call again.'

'It was very clever of you to do so. How did you arrange it?'

'Oh, ways and means, you know,' he replied airily. 'Of course, I have also been busy getting myself kitted out, as you see,' he continued, changing the subject.

'You look very fine, I must say.'

'Oh, fine feathers, you know. And, speaking of fine feathers, permit me to tell you that you look entirely beautiful tonight.'

'Well, I do think I look pretty,' she said candidly. 'And I am so glad you are here to see me, for I dare say I shall never look as well again.'

'Don't be too sure of that. They say all brides look beautiful on their wedding day,' he whispered for her ear alone.

She blushed a fiery red. 'You should not say such things to me now, Robert. Or I suppose I should call you "Mr

Roberts" in company, should I not? At least for the present.'

'No, I think "Sir Robert" would be better. That is the name I gave at the door.'

She looked at him in horror. 'Oh, dear, was that wise? The impropriety of our meeting in the country will be forgiven by my parents, in time, but I do not think that such a deception would please Papa at all.'

Robert thought furiously. The middle of a crowded ballroom was certainly not the place for the explanation that should, that must be made. More than ever he regretted the misunderstanding between them. He knew his betrothed's alarming candour too well to suppose that she would accept her own deception meekly. He shook his head helplessly. 'You must trust me, dearest. I am doing what I think to be best.'

Such masterly tactics might have worked with the biddable Amanda, but Harriet was still disposed to argue. 'That is all very well, but . . .'

Robert made haste to distract her. 'There is a young man over there glaring at us in a most alarming fashion. Is he another of your rejected suitors? Should I fly for my life? He is rather larger than the nameless one.'

She giggled, following his glance. 'Silly, that is only my brother Harry. Viscount St Erth, you know. Will you come and meet him?'

'I scarcely dare to. He looks as if he would like to eat me. How could I have incurred his displeasure so soon?' The horrid suspicion occurred to him that Harriet might have confided in her brother, which might necessitate a painful explanation. He was relieved to hear her exclaim,

'Oh, no, it is not you he is angry with. I am afraid those black looks are for me. The fact is, we had a little disagreement this afternoon, when he arrived.'

'So soon? He is up at Oxford, is he not?'

'Yes, and came down for my ball—so he says, but he admitted to me he wanted to come to London, and this was a good excuse.' She spoke tranquily. This, then, was not the reason for their quarrel.

'Do you generally disagree so violently? Am I to find myself married to a shrew?'

'Not at all,' she replied indignantly. 'We are the best of good friends, and always have been. It is just that he told me something that I did not like, and I am afraid I spoke my mind to him.'

'No, did you? How unusual.'

She shook her head at him in mock displeasure. 'Sir, you are uncivil! He was not very pleased, and I am afraid he had been drinking too much champagne, so now, of course, he is spoiling for a fight.'

'But not with you, I hope? At least, not now.'

'No, for he knows it would not do. That is what makes him so cross, I suppose, for in general he has the most cheerful disposition. He has got himself into a scrape, and I told him what I thought he should do. I am surprised he did not agree with me. I am sure you would have thought me right.'

Casting his mind rapidly over the sort of scrapes a young blood up at Oxford might have got himself into, Robert was not altogether surprised that Harriet's advice had not been appropriate. His sympathies were entirely with the boy. 'I do not think you should tell me anymore,' he warned her. 'He might not like his affairs to be discussed with a stranger.'

'But you are not a stranger, but practically a member of the family. Why, you will be his brother! There can be no possible objection.' Before he could stop her, Harriet was pouring into his ears the saga of St Erth and the lovely, if low-born, Annie.

'And so I told him, he must of course marry her,' she concluded.

'I am afraid your parents might have something to say about that,' he said drily. It was not, after all, an uncommon story. A young man of good name, lured into an indiscretion, however harmless, by a beautiful girl—he was pretty sure that money, rather than marriage, was the aim in view. He had not bargained for Harriet's own natural sense of fair play, now made extra sensitive by her own unconventional love affair.

'How can you say such a thing, you of all people?' she said to him reproachfully. 'Just because she is not—not nobly born! Or even rich! If she is good, and beautiful, and truly loves him, why should he cast her aside?'

'My dear, I am afraid she may love only his name, and his riches.'

'He is not rich! He will inherit the estate, I know, but there is very little money.'

'Not rich by your standards, but to a shop-girl from Oxford, such a match would be quite above her station.'

'Like ours?' she queried in a low, trembling voice.

'Not at all like ours,' he said gently. 'There can be no comparison.'

'I am sorry. That was a dreadful thing to say.'

He clasped her hand reassuringly. 'My dearest love, there is nothing to forgive. Nothing you could say on such a subject could possibly wound me. Only you must believe that in some things I, and even Harry, are wiser than you. Come, let me see you smile, for the dance is nearly over. Your next partner will be looking for you.'

'I do not want to dance with anyone else. Can I not continue to dance with you?'

'That would set tongues wagging, and no mistake! One more dance later, if I may. And, tomorrow, I shall call here again, on your father. You may guess for what purpose.'

She was radiant again, and he watched her being borne away by another young man. Across the room St Erth was still glowering at his sister. Robert gave a small sigh. It looked as though he might need to take up his brotherly duties very soon, before his beloved pushed her brother into a disastrous marriage.

CHAPTER ELEVEN

THE FOLLOWING morning brought Robert to Grosvenor Square. He did not make the mistake of calling at too early an hour: it would not do to find that the ladies of the house were still abed. Controlling his impatience, he walked round the square once to give himself time to arrange his thoughts, then knocked and was admitted. On asking for the Earl, he was shown into the library.

'I will tell his lordship you are here,' said the butler, concealing a burning curiosity under his impassive expression. Always watchful where the family were concerned, he well remembered the gentleman's chagrin on finding, some days before, that the ladies were not at home. It had not escaped his notice that Lady Harriet had greeted Sir Robert with unusual warmth the previous evening, nor had he missed her ecstatic expression as they danced. Such a prompt call argued a romance, and Robert would have been astonished had he known how much sympathetic approval was warming the butler's heart.

Robert turned from his blind contemplation of the books on the library shelves as the Earl entered.

'Atherington? Good morning. Here last night, weren't you?'

'Good morning, my lord. Yes, Lady Cornelia was kind enough to send me a card of invitation. I believe my great-aunt, Lady Beatrice Fitzpaine, mentioned my name to her.

I am lately returned from the Crimea, and find I have few acquaintance in town.'

'Yes, I believe my wife did mention something of the matter to me. Out there, were you? Bad business, by all accounts. Glad to see you here, my dear chap. We must do our best for our returning heroes.'

'As to that, I do not think I can qualify for heroic status, my lord. But I have come to ask you for something that seems to me the best, the most important, thing in the world.'

'Have you indeed? And what might that best and important thing be?'

'I have the honour, my lord,' said Robert, becoming remarkably formal in the solemnity of the moment, 'to ask you for the hand of your daughter, Lady Harriet.'

The Earl was stunned. 'Have you indeed?' He looked at Robert as if he feared that he might suddenly run amok among the books.

'I realise that this request might seem a trifle sudden,' said Robert carefully. He had thought overnight that he should perhaps wait until he and Harriet had been seen to meet a few more times. That, he knew, was the counsel of sense. His heart, however, told him otherwise. Also, knowing Harriet's open nature, he did not think that the secret of their previous friendship could be kept for more than a few minutes.

'A trifle sudden! I should think it does! Why, you only met the girl last night, didn't you? It's an important decision to make on the strength of a couple of dances and one evening with a girl at her come-out ball. I am surprised that a man of your experience should do such a thing. My advice to you is to go home and sleep it off.'

Robert had to smile. He could hardly blame his host for his very natural supposition. 'My lord, I am not drunk. I have to tell you that I am already acquainted with Lady Harriet. This is no sudden decision on my part.'

'Know her already, do you? Met since she came up to London, perhaps?'

'No, my lord. Our acquaintance dates from before then. It is not so very long, but long enough for me to be quite sure that I could never be happy with any other, and I flatter myself that the lady feels the same way.'

The Earl looked at him suspiciously.

'That's all very well, but how is it you come to have met her in the country? I'm sure I've never seen you before in my life, and I don't believe my wife has, either. I have to tell you that we saw the way you two were looking at one another last night, and she made no mention of a previous acquaintanceship. That being the case, I find it hard to understand how it is you have spent time with my daughter.'

Robert braced himself. 'I have to beg your indulgence, my lord, if what I am about to tell you should in any way shock you, and I beg also that it will not give you a disgust of me. In plain words, I have for some weeks past been the guest of Mr and Mrs Johnson.'

'What—the Johnsons at Home Farm? But that young man was a plain Mr—I forget the name, but it was certainly not Atherington, which is the name you claim to bear at present.' The Earl's brows were bristling with suspicion, and Robert regretted, once again, that he had ever allowed himself to behave in what, with hindsight, looked so underhand a fashion.

'I regret to say, my lord, that I did not reveal my identity to your tenants, and to that extent I was with them under false pretences,' he said stiffly. 'I must explain that I have inherited, while I was out of the country, the estate and title of my cousin Arthur Atherington.' He could not feel that his late relative's reputation was likely to enhance his own, and continued before the Earl had time to say anything. 'On returning from the Crimea I visited the estate, and was very shocked to find how run-down it was. The state of the house, not to mention the land, and the conditions in which the labourers live, were all in a very poor way. I was determined to do what I could to improve things. There was no lack of means—my own father left me very well provided for, and my cousin was also a wealthy man, though he did not choose to spend his money.'

The Earl nodded. This much he knew from local gossip, and from what the Countess had heard from Lady Beatrice. At least his daughter's suitor—if he was indeed the man he said he was—was a man of good standing, and the farmer in him envied the opportunity he now had. 'That's all very right and fine, but why come sneaking in under an assumed name? You must know that I would have been happy to let you visit and learn from our farms. I rather pride myself we have a good system there, and I'm glad to teach anyone who wants to learn from it.'

'Indeed, my lord,' responded Robert warmly, 'I was told by my own tenant that your estate is run on the most modern lines, and that I could not do better than study it.'

'So why all the secrecy?'

'It is hard to explain, though at the time I saw no harm, for I expected to meet no one but your tenant and his men. I should tell you that I returned from the Crimea not only wounded, though that is now healed, but also deeply shocked and depressed by what I had seen there. I found myself out of tune with society, and for a while unable to enjoy its pleasures.' He looked at the Earl, who grunted. 'In short, my lord, I wanted time to heal my spirit, and it seemed to me that a period of labouring among simple, country people would be the best cure. I did not intend to mislead you or your family, for I did not expect ever to meet them. I wanted to live as the farmer did, and work as he did. I knew that if he had known my true position in life he would never allow me to do this, at least not properly.'

A simple man himself, the Earl could appreciate the honesty of this reply. 'But you did meet Harriet?'

'Yes, by accident. But there I hold myself to blame, and I know you can only be shocked by my conduct. I am afraid I did not tell the lady my true identity. At first there seemed no need, for I thought we would never see each other again, and I did not think anything of it. Then, when we met a few times more I found that I did not want to. I have to tell you that at that time nothing was further from my mind than love, or marriage. We talked as chance acquaintances, and later as friends. I need hardly tell you that nothing of an improper nature passed between us.'

'So I should hope! And you met in secret? Well, that was very wrong, and I do not know what Lady Cornelia would say about it, but I suppose no harm is done.'

'I hope not, my lord. We met as friends, and I learned to value that friendship too much to put it at risk by telling Lady Harriet my true identity. You must know well her own open nature, and how she shrinks from dishonesty and falsehood. By the time our friendship had grown into love, I did not know how to tell her.'

'And now you are resolved upon marriage?'

'Most firmly resolved, and I am sure that Lady Harriet loves me as truly as I love her.'

'So I must suppose. How did she take it when you told her the truth?'

'I am afraid I have not yet told her.'

The Earl was dumbfounded.

'Not told her? How is this?'

'Our last meeting was so short, and she was so hurried, that though I started to explain she gave me no time. I have not seen her from that moment until last night, and I could not feel that it was the right time for such an explanation.'

'I should think not, indeed! Well, here is a pretty kettle of fish, and no mistake: You had better see her at once, young man, and make your peace with her. I suppose I can only give my consent to the marriage, if you are both so set on it. It seems suitable enough. No, don't thank me yet! I'll send her down to you, and explain things to Lady Cornelia as best I may. You'd better leave me to do that, don't you think? She'll come round, soon enough, once everything is settled.'

Leaving the library and his guest, the Earl trod heavily up to his wife's sitting room, not choosing to employ the butler in this delicate affair. He found Lady Cornelia and Harriet together. His daughter looked up hopefully as he entered.

'Well, puss,' he said jovially, 'there's a young man downstairs who would like a few words with you.' He gave a laugh as she jumped to her feet, blushing vividly.

'Oh, Papa! You are not displeased?'

'Displeased? I hardly know; there hasn't been time to think of it. He's given me the tale openly though, I will say, and if it's what you want, my dear...'

'It is, Papa, oh, it is!' she cried, running to embrace him and whisking out of the room before he could do more than return her kiss. Then he turned to his astonished wife, and set himself to reveal as much of the story as he thought suitable, for the time being.

Harriet ran down to the library, then entered rather shyly. This was very different from the stolen meetings in the woods, which had for the most part been in a spirit of innocent friendship. Now she received Robert as an acknowledged lover, with her father's blessing, in the formality of the library.

Robert looked up as she entered, and strode towards her. 'My dearest! At last!' he said huskily, as he took her into his arms.

She returned kisses with enthusiasm, then drew away, laughing. 'Come Robert, you should not kiss me until after you have proposed, you know.'

'I thought I had already done that.'

'But that was different. Now we have Papa's consent, and we can be properly betrothed.'

Half jesting, half in earnest, he went on one knee to her. 'Lady Harriet, will you do me the great honour of accepting my hand and my heart?'

'But, sir, this is so sudden,' she said in joking coyness, then protested laughingly as he caught her in his arms again. 'Very well, I shall. But tell me, Robert, for I am dying to know, how did you talk Papa round so quickly? I was sure he would not give his permission straight away. Did you tell him everything?'

He led her to a small sofa, and obliged her to sit down, seating himself close to her, and holding her tightly to him with one arm. He resolved to speak out boldly.

'The fact is, my dear, that I was able to show him that I am an eligible suitor. As Mr Roberts, he would probably have me kicked out of the house, but as Sir Robert Atherington, owner of a fine estate some thirty miles from your home, I was a different proposition.'

'But Robert, when he finds out the truth he will never forgive you! And you cannot keep up such a pretence for long, you know. Particularly when Atherington is so near. Why did you not say Yorkshire, or Scotland, if you had to make up a tale. Yet I cannot understand how you could be so foolish as to attempt it, or how you should have thought I would allow it.'

'Because it is the truth, my dearest, and no pretence. I really am Sir Robert Atherington.' He knew she must be surprised, even shocked, and did not wonder when she withdrew from his arm and sat stiffly beside him.

'How can this be? Mrs Johnson...'

'Mrs Johnson did not know. I called myself Roberts with them, because I did not wish to be obliged to take up my position in society. I have to tell you that when I first took up residence at Atherington Hall I was much sought after by the matchmaking mamas!'

He had hoped to make her smile, but she took him all too seriously.

'So you feared that Mama would throw me at your head! I wonder that you dared speak to me at all, if you thought me so predatory. Why, then, did you meet with me, and encourage me to be your friend?'

'Because I liked you, first of all, and very soon I learned to love you.'

'But you did not tell me the truth.'

Her voice was flat and cold, and she would not look at him.

'Darling girl, I am so sorry. I know I should have done. But at first there was no thought of love between us, and I must admit it was pleasant—to be Mr Roberts, and to feel that you liked me for myself, and not for my estate and money.'

She rose to her feet proudly. 'We are not rich, I know, but I would never have been influenced by your wealth,' she said in revolted tones.

'I know it! But by the time I realised I had fallen in love with you, so much time had gone by that I did not know how to tell you that I was not Mr Roberts, but Sir Robert.

The thought that you were prepared to brave all, to give up all, for me, was so inexpressibly dear to me. And I truly tried to tell you, that last day, but you gave me no time. Nor could I tell you in the middle of your first ball. Please try to understand how it was!'

'I understand that you were prepared to accept all I offered, any sacrifice, which would have been no sacrifice to me because I loved you. You revelled in that knowledge, and did not give me the truth in return.' He tried to take her into his arms again, but she slipped away from him, keeping her face averted so that he would not see the tears that spilled from her eyes.

'No, Sir Robert,' she said in that new, cold little voice. 'You did not want to be pestered by young ladies wishing to ally themselves with your fortune. So you tested me, and when you found that I passed your medieval test, then you deign to think of bestowing that fortune upon me.'

'It is not like that at all, Harriet,' he said angry now himself at her stinging words. Though he would not admit it, there was an element of truth in her words, although his actions had never been so calculated. 'Dearest girl,' he said more calmly, taking her hand once again and forcing her to turn towards him. 'Do not weep. I have offended, and I beg your forgiveness. I have told your father, and he for one has no objection to our marriage. Can you not be glad of that?'

'Objection! He has no objection! But I have,' she cried, now quite beyond all rational thought. 'I have objection. It was Mr Roberts that I loved, and for whom I was prepared to brave my parents' anger. Not Sir Robert Atherington! I do not know you. You are a stranger to me. Oh, I never want to see you again!'

Before he could say another word, she had pulled her hand free from his hold, and run from the room, slamming the door behind her.

CHAPTER TWELVE

HURRYING UP the stairs, her eyes blinded by tears, Harriet almost collided with the Earl and Countess who, hearing her footsteps, were hastening from the little upstairs sitting room.

'Hold hard! What are those tears, then, child? It is a little late for such missish behaviour now, surely. You have had your explanation with Sir Robert, I suppose?'

'Oh, Papa,' sobbed Harriet, almost unable to speak. 'Do not reproach me now, for you cannot know how I repent of my behaviour.'

'Repent? Yes, of course, but it seems to me it has all turned out very well.'

Harriet turned reproachful eyes on her father. 'How can you say so, Papa? I am so unhappy!'

'What have you got to be unhappy about? You've just become engaged to the feller. Thought from what he said you were mad for each other. You looked happy enough a minute ago, when you went downstairs.'

'Engaged! No such thing,' cried Harriet.

'Do you mean to tell me, Harriet,' said the Countess in a voice of dangerous calm, 'that you, having behaved with an impropriety that I can hardly believe any child of mine could contemplate, have now refused the offer of a gentleman who, as well as being in possession of an ample fortune and a handsome person, also appears to love you to distraction?'

'Yes,' said Harriet baldly.

'Refused him? You must have a maggot in your brain, girl,' stormed her father, who, while she had been downstairs had learned from his wife, more *au fait* than he with country gossip and possessed of an extra source of information in Lady Beatrice, exactly how great was the inheritance into which Robert had lately come.

Harriet could only hang her head and sob. The Countess, seeing that harsh words would avail nothing, subdued her own dismay and tried to comfort her daughter.

'It is all very upsetting for you, to be sure, but this can be no more than a lovers' quarrel,' she said soothingly, gathering Harriet to her. 'If I thought you were indifferent to him, no considerations of fortune would bring me to encourage you into this match. But your father assures me this is not the case, and indeed, Harriet, your feelings were plain to see only last night, and this morning.'

'But I didn't know then,' wailed Harriet. 'Oh, Mama, he has deceived me!'

'Deceived you! If he had pretended to be Sir Robert, when he was merely a farmer, then indeed you would have been deceived. But I am at a loss to see, dear Harriet, how you can be other than delighted to find that he is so eligible a suitor. You must have known that Papa and I would have been very unwilling to consent to so unequal a match, at least for some years.'

'Yes, and I was prepared for that,' said her recalcitrant daughter. 'I cannot explain why I mind so much, Mama. It is only that I thought I had found a friend, someone I could trust in all things. If he lied to me about this, what else might be false? I should never be able to trust him.'

Seeing that the Earl was looking almost apoplectic with wrath, Lady Cornelia shook her head at him, and started to lead Harriet away to her bedchamber. 'Come, my love, you are overwrought. You have had a very exciting few days, and very little sleep last night, and I know you must be tired. One cannot see things clearly in such a state. Come and rest now, and see if things do not seem better tomorrow.' Over her shoulder she gave the Earl a forceful nod towards the stairs. 'Do you go down, my lord, and speak to the young man.'

'I shall not change my mind. I shall never forgive him, never!' With these last defiant words, Harriet suffered herself to be led away.

The Earl entered the library gloomily, where he found Robert pacing the room with a thunderous expression. 'Taken it badly, hasn't she? I was afraid she might, you know. Very high spirited girl. Always was. Gets it from her mother, you know.'

'There is no good in my staying here. I will wish you a good morning, my lord.'

'Steady on, steady on! You're as bad as she is, damn it all. Girls get funny notions at times like this, you know. Friend of mine was refused three times before she accepted him, and told him afterwards that she meant to have him all the time! Fact!'

'That is not the kind of behaviour I would have expected from Lady Harriet. Tell me, my lord, how many times can you recall her changing her mind, once it was made up?'

The Earl looked doubtful. 'Not often, I must say. But she's had a shock, you know. She'll come round. Besides, you might say she already has changed her mind, deciding she doesn't love you after all. Just as likely to change it back again.'

'Lady Harriet has made her sentiments abundantly clear to me,' said Robert bitterly. 'She said that I am not the man she fell in love with, and therefore she does not love me.'

'Well, at least stay in town for a while,' begged the Earl. 'Don't go burying yourself in the country, or taking up residence somewhere else in another name.'

It was not a tactful reminder.

'That, at least, is something I am never likely to do again,' said Robert even more bitterly. 'I fancy I have learned my lesson about that.'

He turned to leave. The door opened almost in his face and Harry burst in.

'I say, Father, what on earth's going on? Oh, excuse me, sir,' he added to Robert. 'I thought my father was alone. I will go.'

'Not on my account, St Erth. I am just leaving.'

'Sir Robert Atherington, my son Viscount St Erth,' said the Earl with automatic civility.

Harry shook Robert's hand with more than a little curiosity. 'How do you do, Sir Robert? I saw you last night, did I not, dancing with my sister? She seemed mighty taken with you.'

'You did, St Erth. I am afraid it is not a sight you are ever likely to see again. Good morning!' And on this unencouraging note, he left.

Harry stared at his father. 'What was all that about? Did I say something wrong?'

The Earl turned to the tantalus as a camel in the desert heads for an oasis.

'May I offer you some brandy, Harry?' he asked gloomily. 'That was the most eligible suitor Harriet is ever likely to entertain, and she refused him.'

'Refused him? I don't understand. When I saw them together last night you could have lit a candle at her eyes, and he wasn't much different, either.'

The Earl, needing someone to share his troubles as well as his brandy, explained to his heir the morning's happenings.

'I see,' said Harry thoughtfully, absent-mindedly refilling his glass and that of his father. 'Well, that explains it.' He fell into a brown study, and the pair of them sat silently sipping. Harry, for one, now understood in part at least why his sister had been so vehement in her insistence that he should marry Annie. He wondered whether she would have changed her opinion now. His father just wondered, generally, whether any man could understand the way a woman's mind worked.

At length Harry roused himself. 'Don't worry, father. I'll see what I can do to help,' he said rather grandly.

The Earl, who might once have resented his tone, was not above clutching at straws. 'Very good of you, my boy. Very grateful. She's always been fond of you. Perhaps you can make her see reason. By the way, shouldn't you be back at Oxford?'

'And leave you all in the lurch? I wouldn't dream of it. Besides, important family affairs, you know! I'll make it all right with my tutor later.'

His father raised suspicious eyebrows, wise in the ways of young men at university. 'In debt, are you?'

'Certainly not, sir—at least, not to be worth mentioning. I gave you my word!' said his son indignantly.

'I beg your pardon, St Erth.' The Earl spoke with unwonted meekness. 'Yes, you speak to her. At all events, it can't make things any worse than they are.'

On this optimistic note, they parted.

IT WAS NOT until much later in the day that Harry was allowed to speak to his sister. As Lady Cornelia had expected, Harriet soon sobbed herself into a restless sleep.

The Countess covered her with a shawl, and left with instruction to her maid to stay with her, and summon her when Lady Harriet should awake. Harriet slept for several hours, and woke with a heavy head and eyes puffed and sore from crying. At her mother's insistence she took some soup, and a little bread and butter.

'Now, my dear, we shall have a comfortable talk,' said Lady Cornelia hopefully. A talk they had, but it was not comfortable. Harriet confided in her mother the full tale of what had happened. Lady Cornelia was shocked at the meetings in the woods, for the Earl had seen fit to skate over their number and duration in his explanations to her. Wisely, she hid her feelings. She found it hard, however, to enter into her daughter's sentiments on the deception. Her older, more conventional ideas could not accept that a marriage with a man out of one's own class, however gentlemanly, could be truly happy. When Harry came in she was relieved to leave Harriet with him, since her own counsels availed nothing.

'You see, Harry, I am in a scrape, too,' said Harriet with a watery smile when they were alone. 'I fear that mine is not as easily resolved as yours, though.'

'Now, Hetty, you must not talk like that. I wish I had never told you about Annie—it is you we must think of now.'

'On the contrary,' she said with great energy. 'I have made up my mind that I shall never marry. I shall stay at home, and be a comfort to Mama and Papa. You, on the other hand, are in quite a different case.'

Harry thought that the chances of Mama or Papa being at all comforted by their eldest daughter's remaining at home were all but non-existent, when she could have had what amounted to a brilliant marriage, but wisely held his tongue on that subject. With what he felt was almost fiendish cunning, he framed another innocent enquiry. 'This Sir Robert of yours is rolling in money, isn't he?' Harriet's strong brows drew together in a frown. 'Only I was just thinking, if you were to marry him, my father would perhaps not mind so much about Annie. Of course, they would like me to find a girl with a handsome dowry, and of good family, but if you were to marry well . . .' His voice trailed off suggestively.

Harriet looked at him with reproach. 'I could not do that, even for you, Harry. I am sure you would not expect it.'

'But, dash it all, I'm not trying to sell you into slavery! Last night you looked at him as if he were the only man in the world. You cannot have changed your feelings that much, in twelve hours!'

'Last night,' Harriet sighed. 'Last night I did not know how he had deceived me. Do not, I beg of you, tease me, Harry. I am so unhappy. I thought you, of all people, would understand. Imagine if your Annie had dealt so with you!'

For a moment Harry contemplated the unlikely possibility of discovering that Annie was really a wealthy duchess in disguise. His imagination, he found, was not equal to the task. He also learned something else—that if such an unlikely thing were to happen, it would not make him any more eager to marry her. He reflected that he had, in a sense, been as much deceived as Harriet, for to his recollection no word of marriage had ever been suggested by him to his erstwhile inamorata. Her father's claims were made on the vague poetic wishes and hopes expressed in the stanzas he had penned in the first heat of romantic passion.

It was obvious, however, that Harriet was unwilling to talk about her own affairs, and Harry at length decided to

humour her. She seemed eager to know every detail of his
first meeting with Annie, where she worked, how she
looked, and feeling that it was a good idea to distract her
for a while from her own troubles, he obliged her with a
full account, first to last. It did not bring him any nearer
solving his own difficulties, or helping hers, but it was
rather flattering that she was so interested. It did not occur to him that there could be any harm in answering all
her questions, even when she wanted to know Annie's
surname, and where she lived. At the end of an hour he felt
he could say that he had cheered her out of her misery, and
was blissfully unaware that Harriet was already formulat-
ing plans for his future that would have horrified him if he
had known them.

THEY WERE to have dined with friends, and gone to the
Opera, but Lady Cornelia sent to say that Harriet was a
little indisposed, being rather overtired with the excite-
ments of the previous night. She felt she could place no
reliance on her daughter's behaving in a ladylike fashion
if, by a mischance, they should encounter her former lover
in the corridors of Covent Garden.

All in all, Harriet felt beleaguered. The only person who
remotely understood how she felt was Amanda. Admitted
to her sister's confidence, Amanda had entered in full into
every feeling. Knowing her sister's fierce and uncompro-
mising honesty in everything, she could quite see how
Harriet must feel. At the same time, though, it did seem a
shame that Harriet, having found someone who shared her
own interests, and whose way of life was so very agreeable
to her, should refuse to see him again. Wiser than her parents and brother, she said nothing of this. While Harriet
had almost never been known to change her mind on any
important issue, she was above all very fair. Amanda felt

that the best hope for a reconciliation might be to bring Harriet to feel that she had been unjust and hasty in making that decision.

Amanda contented herself with commiserating, and listening, and the whispered conversation continued far into the night. Without attempting to change her sister's mind for her, she contrived to present Robert's case as she saw it, from his side, and to convince Harriet that he had acted, as he saw it, in good faith. She could not feel that she had made any great progress, but at least Harriet did not decline to listen to her, which was something.

CHAPTER THIRTEEN

THE FOLLOWING morning Lady Cornelia, presiding as was her wont over the family breakfast table, looked with exasperation at her two eldest daughters. A strong-minded woman, she had been brought up to a strict observation of the duties of her position in life, in which she included setting a good example to the lower orders in the matter of early rising. Breakfast in bed, except in times of illness, she considered to be a waste of servants' time and an unnecessary self-indulgence. No excuse of a late night or lack of sleep would be allowed as a reason to lie abed beyond eight o'clock. Any late night should be prepared for by proper resting the afternoon before.

The Earl and Countess therefore had the doubtful felicity of seeing their three eldest offspring, all pale and lacking in appetite, gracing the matutinal table. The Earl, having piled his plate with cold sirloin, was obliviously working his way through it, plastering each mouthful with mustard and demanding frequent refills of his coffee cup. Between mouthfuls he kept his eyes firmly fixed on a pamphlet that had just been published on the subject of roots, and from long experience Lady Cornelia knew that he was going to deal with the family problems in his usual way, which was to ignore them until someone else, probably herself, sorted them out.

For a moment her eyes rested fondly on her eldest son who was, though she would never have admitted it, her favourite child. She had ordered devilled kidneys, knowing them to be his favourite, and he had dutifully taken some and was now listlessly pushing them around his plate. If she had not had her mind on Harriet this might have worried her, but knowing that he had spent much of the night out drinking with friends she was not unduly disturbed.

Her gaze returned to her daughters. Amanda, earlier admonished by her mother to eat something, was dutifully consuming a boiled egg, keeping her eyes fixed on her plate and occasionally wiping away a sympathetic tear. Harriet, dry eyed, had pushed her egg away. Over-cooked, the dry morsels of yolk stuck like glue to her palate and were impossible to swallow. Her face, thought her mother crossly, looked positively sallow. Whatever had happened to the blooming damsel who had danced at the ball only the night before last? Lady Cornelia sighed, and tried to subdue her rising irritation.

'If you are not going to eat that egg, Harriet, then please make an effort to take some bread and butter.'

'Yes, Mama.' Harriet's tone was lifeless, and she obediently pushed the egg further away and took a slice of bread.

'You will feel better when you have eaten,' continued the Countess in gentler tones. 'I will give you another cup of tea.'

'Yes, Mama. Thank you, Mama.'

For once, Lady Cornelia was at a loss. She was accustomed to worrying about Harriet. She had been doing it for years. She was accustomed, fond of her though she was, to finding her irritating. But never, in all those years, had she felt so unsure of herself. Looking back on her own girlhood and courtship she could find nothing in her own experience to help her to understand her daughter's attitude. No one who had seen the couple together on the night of the Ball could doubt that they were in love, and yet here was the headstrong girl, faced with a suitor who was not only acceptable but highly desirable, refusing to have him because he was not the poor farmer she had thought him. If Harriet had been a silly, romantic girl allowed to read foolish novels it would have been more understandable, but Harriet had always been so practical, so down to earth. She knew, although it had never been openly discussed between them, that it was important for her to make as good a marriage as possible, and help to launch her sisters when the time came.

The bread and butter, undiminished in volume, was crumbled on the plate. Harriet sat stiffly upright, while Amanda drooped over her unfinished egg. Lady Cornelia felt that she could not bear to look at them any longer, nor could she find anything useful to say to them. A short period of separation would, she felt, be beneficial to them all.

'I think a little fresh air, girls, would be good for you both. It promises to be a fine day. Miss Jeremy has been wanting to take a day off to visit her cousin in Kensington, so you may take the children to the park for the morning. St Erth, if your father permits you to absent yourself from Oxford for a few days, you may escort them.'

Her firm tone brooked no denial. Harriet and Amanda obediently rose from the table, and St Erth with equal alacrity opened the door, and followed them out into the hall. He looked sulky.

'If that isn't the limit! If I had known I would be spending my time playing nursemaid to a parcel of brats, dashed if I wouldn't have stayed in Oxford.'

Harriet opened her mouth to remind him just why he had not wished to stay in Oxford, then remembered that her sister knew nothing of the matter, and closed it again. She then bethought her of a few other home truths that she might offer, but Amanda, seeing storm signals on the horizon, forestalled her before she could do more than draw breath.

'I know it is disagreeable for you, Harry, but it would be so good of you to come. I will try not to let the little ones bother you, but I think Mama is right that some time out of doors will refresh us all. And to go with you, instead of Miss Jeremy, will be such a treat!' She squeezed his arm and smiled at him with artless flattery, and he could not but be softened.

'Well, if the children behave, I don't mind,' he said gruffly. 'And you two girls will be better protected with a man to escort you.'

'As if we were planning to wander around Blackheath,' whispered Amanda to Harriet as their brother ran upstairs. 'But it will be pleasanter with Harry than with Miss Jeremy, for she never stops talking and still treats me as a schoolgirl.'

'I hate walking in the park; there are too many people,' said Harriet, hardly hearing her sister's words. 'How I wish I were back in the country.'

'I know, dearest,' soothed Amanda. 'We shall keep to the less frequented paths, and maybe we shall not meet anyone we know.'

The Earl, meanwhile, had conceived a plan of what seemed to him to be Machiavellian ingenuity. Without consulting with his wife, who might have disabused him, he hastened from the breakfast room to the study, where he scribbled a few lines to Robert, informing him of Harriet's whereabouts and suggesting that he contrive to meet her, as if by chance. He also gave him the information that Harriet was very unhappy, and might be regretting the events of yesterday. Folding the note, he scrawled Robert's name on the outside and rang his bell. When the butler entered the Earl thrust the note at him.

'I want this taken at once, Crowborough—at once, mind you—and delivered to Sir Robert Atherington. Without delay,' he added, just to be quite sure that he had made himself clear.

'Very good, my lord. Is my lord acquainted with Sir Robert's address?'

The Earl looked blank.

'His address? Of course I'm not. Dash it all, now what are we to do?'

Crowborough rose to the occasion with his usual aplomb. 'It is of no consequence, my lord. I recollect that her ladyship sent the gentleman a card of invitation to the ball. His address will be on her list.'

A look of alarm crossed the Earl's face. 'Fact is, this is a private matter, Crowborough. Something her ladyship doesn't need to know about, just yet, don't you see.'

The butler, who had a burning curiosity to know what was causing all the upset in the household, was eager to help. 'Leave it to me, my lord,' he said soothingly. 'I shall see that your letter is delivered as quickly as possible, without, er, bothering her ladyship.'

Robert was at home when the letter arrived, which was fortunate as it had not crossed the Earl's rather one-tracked mind that he might not be. Barton, wooden-faced, carried the letter up to his master and proffered it silently. Robert, leaving his lodgings the day before in the best of spirits, had returned later in the day in a towering rage. After having had his head bitten off three times for venturing quite ordinary remarks, Barton had taken refuge in dignified silence. He was aware that Robert had paced the floor half the night, and had had no appetite for his breakfast. He felt he had a fairly good idea of the reason, and was not unduly worried. He could not believe that any girl in her right mind would seriously mean to refuse so eligible a match as his master, and thought privately that she was merely playing the coquette.

Robert read the note once, frowning, and then again more slowly. It went to his heart to think that Harriet was unhappy, but wiser than the Earl, he was not at all sure that to meet Harriet in the park was a good idea. She had had, he felt, very little time to come to terms with her new knowledge of him, and he had little relish for a scene in public, under the interested eyes of her brothers and sisters. Knowing her as he did, he placed little reliance on her ability to hide her feelings even in so public a place. Nevertheless, the temptation to see her again proved too strong. He felt sure that if only he could talk to her, persuade her to listen to him, he would be able to convince her. He had no doubt of her love for him, and he could not believe that she could seriously doubt his for her. Somehow, he must make her see that he was, indeed, the same man she loved, that for her he was still Mr Roberts of nowhere in particular.

To arrange a chance meeting in Hyde Park on a fine morning in early summer, when half of London seemed to be out taking the air, was by no means as easy as the Earl had fondly hoped. Robert soon realised, after he had gone through the gates and seen how almost every path was thronged with people, that it would indeed be the sheerest luck if he succeeded in finding Harriet at all, let alone in separating her from her escort and having a quiet conversation. The opportunity was too good to miss, however, so he set off at a determined stride down the first path that led towards the Serpentine. Inexperienced though he was in the ways of children, he felt sure that the lure of water would exercise its usual fascination over the young, and lead them in that direction.

He reached the near side of the lake without seeing anyone he knew. Scanning the paths, and then the opposite shore, his heart sank. There were parties of children, in charge of their nurses or their governesses, all around. Several times he thought he had seen the group he sought, but every time a closer look showed him that Harriet was not among them. Still looking, but trying not to be too obvious in his search, he continued along the path by the lake.

So intent was he that he failed to notice a familiar face in the crowds. Even the sound of his own name being called failed to arrest him, and it was not until he felt his arm grasped and held that he stopped and turned.

'Robert! Why, Robert Atherington! Or, should I say, Sir Robert? Dash it, man, have you grown so proud that you don't speak to your friends any more?'

Robert looked down into the blue eyes of one of his greatest friends, whose severe words were belied by the delighted grin that split his face beneath the familiar snub nose.

'Barney! By all that's wonderful! I had no thought of meeting you here. I thought you were in Scotland.'

'So I was, my boy, so I was. Doing the pretty to all the relatives, and deuced uncomfortable it was, too. So, of course, when I heard that my old friend and companion in crime had returned from being a hero, I upped and went. Can't let my oldest friend show himself to society without someone to tell him how to go on. You know you could never manage without me!'

They had been friends since their schooldays, and Barney Ashstead probably knew Robert better than any man alive, except Barton. The blue eyes that scanned his face missed very little, though he continued to rattle on in his usual inconsequential manner.

'Made yourself unpopular with your grandmother, I suppose?' asked Robert cynically. Barney's grandmother, an irascible octogenarian of reputedly fabulous wealth, was at once the bane and the saviour of Barney's existence. She could generally be relied on to extricate him from the worst of his financial problems, but only at the cost of interminable visits spent playing cribbage, and brushing her ancient and smelly dog.

'Not at all,' Barney retorted loftily. 'As a matter of fact she's very pleased with me. Very pleased indeed. In fact, now that I've settled down, she is making me a regular allowance, and dashed generous it is too. No, we were making our bride visits.' He spoke nonchalantly, and the effect was all that he could have desired.

'Bride visits? Settled down? Barney, can it be that some poor female has taken pity on you at last?'

Barney looked smug. 'Not so much of the taking pity, if you please. You bachelors should show more respect to us married men.'

'But when was this? How is it that I hadn't heard?'

'Some four months ago. I wrote to you in the Crimea, but you must have been on your way home at the time. Fact is, it was all rather sudden. We met at a soirée at the Berringtons'—Lady St Ervan is by way of being a distant relative of mine, you know. I can tell you, Sally just bowled me over. With my irresistible charm she could not but find me equally fascinating, and we were engaged within two weeks. Naturally, I had intended to wait and ask you to be my groomsman, but Sally's father wanted to get back to India, so we just had to carry on without you.'

'Back to India? Barney, can it be that you have married a Nabob's daughter?'

'As a matter of fact, I have!'

'No wonder your grandmother is pleased with you! You old devil, and you with never a penny to fly with! And is she pretty, as well? That seems too much to hope for.'

'I think so,' said his friend simply. 'But you can judge for yourself, in a moment, she is just over there. She was speaking to some old biddy she knows, and I left her sitting on that seat while I ran after you. The fact is,' he blushed slightly, 'that she is in an interesting condition, just now, so I have to take the greatest care of her.'

'My dear fellow, my heartiest congratulations.' Robert seized his friend by the hand and shook it warmly. 'I do wish you every possible happiness. But come, I can wait no longer. Introduce me to your wife, if you please!'

The new Mrs Ashstead proved to be very young, certainly no more than seventeen, Robert thought. Small and plump, she had delightful dimples which instantly appeared when Barney introduced his friend. She held out her hand with a pretty assumption of matronly dignity.

'Sir Robert! How very pleased I am to meet you at last. Barney has told me about you, oh, so much, and I was so sorry that you could not be at our wedding. But naturally, Papa wished to see me married before he left England, so we were, but we drank a toast to you at the breakfast!' She finished her speech in a breathless schoolgirl rush, and Robert, seeing the besotted look on Barney's face, was both amused and touched.

'Then consider me to have been there in spirit, if not in fact. One omission, though, must be rectified immediately. I claim the groomsman's right to kiss the bride!' This he did, and her blush was pretty to behold. 'You fill me with alarm, though, that Barney has told you so much about me. Not all the terrible exploits of our schooldays, I trust?'

The dimples reappeared. 'Some of them, at any rate! But now you shall tell me if they are true or not, and have your revenge on Barney by telling me about him. Will you not walk with us for a while?'

It was impossible to refuse such an invitation. Robert offered her his arm as she rose, while Barney with an anxious solicitude that at any other time would have had Robert teasing him unmercifully, gave her his arm on her other side. Thus escorted the bride walked off, besieged on both sides by banter and reminiscence. Robert, however, had only half his mind on their conversation, and continued to search the faces in the crowd as they walked.

HARRIET, TOO, WAS finding the crowds irksome. She had met so many people since her arrival in London that it was impossible not to encounter someone who knew her. She had never found the inanities of social exchange easy, and today, with her mind quite otherwise, it seemed impossible to smile, to introduce, and to respond to polite enquiries as to the state of her health, her mother's health, her father's health, and her opinion on such theatrical performances as she had seen. Still worse were the endless congratulations on her brilliant ball the day before yesterday. The ball, carrying with it as it did the memory of vanished happiness, was the last thing she wished to think of.

The children, also, found it very boring. Edwina had brought a small book in her pocket, and was surreptitiously reading it whenever the party was brought to a halt by some friend or other. Augusta, John and Isabella, who would not have dreamed of misbehaving with Miss Jeremy, took advantage of Amanda's good nature and Harriet's inattention to fidget, giggle, and tease one another. Harry simply looked gloomy. Although he might be a year older than Harriet, he was beginning to realise that in the eyes of the world she was a young woman, while he was still a boy.

Their fourth meeting, with a voluble matron of ample figure and high colour, ended abruptly. Harry, who had not been attending, was startled to see her sweeping off without so much as a farewell. Amanda looked shocked, while Harriet was biting her lip in embarrassment and looked as though she might burst into tears at any moment.

'What is the matter? Who was the old trout, anyway? She seemed a bit put out.'

'Put out! I should think she was! Oh Harry, it's my fault, I said something I shouldn't, but I completely forgot.' Harriet gave a hysterical giggle. 'It's Mrs Abbotsleigh, you know. She kept on about my ball, and whether I had a beau yet, in that horridly vulgar way, and I was so desperate to stop her that I said the first thing that came into my head. I asked after her son.'

'What's so dreadful about that? Sounds perfectly civil to me. Sort of thing anyone might ask.'

'But, Harry, don't you remember? There was some awful scandal, two or three years ago. I never really understood what it was that he did, but he had to leave the country very quickly, and has never been back. I think he went to Australia. They say that if he had not done he would have gone to prison, or been hanged, or something.'

'Good lord, yes, it had quite slipped my mind,' said Harry. 'I do remember hearing something about it. Didn't the Marquis of Berrington have something to do with it? Still, it's ancient history now, and at least you got rid of her,' he continued practically. 'And ten to one she'll never speak to us again, which will be an even greater gain. What is it, young 'un?' Lady Isabella was tugging at his sleeve, deputed as the youngest to make the requests.

'John says it's awfully slow stuff here, Harry. We have more fun when we come out with Miss Jeremy. Can't we go home?'

'Mama said we should spend the morning in the park,' corrected Amanda gently, seeing that her brother was about to support the younger ones.

'If I have to walk here much longer I shall go into hysterics,' announced Harriet firmly. 'I cannot bear to be among all these people.'

'I think somewhere quieter...' started Amanda.

Augusta interrupted. 'We know a good place in Kensington Gardens—that's the Park too, really. It's further away, but it's much quieter, and there are paths where we can play hide and seek.'

'Then let us go there, by all means.' Harry gallantly offered an arm to each of his sisters, and the younger ones led the way.

It was, as they had said, much less frequented. A nursemaid with her charges, two young couples with eyes only for each other, and some other children, were all they met. Harriet began to relax.

'This is better. I do not think I will ever become used to London. There are altogether too many people.' The children ran off on some game of their own, even Edwina for once putting her book aside and joining the romp. The sisters and brother walked on in silence. They turned a corner of the path, and came upon the interesting spectacle of a man tenderly embracing his female companion, his arm around her waist and his face looking tenderly down into hers. Harry muttered an apology and would have withdrawn in all haste, but beside him Harriet stiffened in outrage and would not be moved.

'Robert!' she said in ringing, shocked tones. The man looked up. In other circumstances Harry would have been amused to see the mixture of surprise, horror and consternation that appeared on his face. He tried hastily to remove his arm from the lady's waist, but she clutched at his coat.

'Harriet! I... You must not think... This is not...' he stammered, surprised out of his usual *savoir faire*. He tried again. 'This is lady is unwell,' he began, but got no further.

'Unwell? I should think she is. And I am sure she deserves to be!' Harriet stifled a sob.

'Come, Harriet, do not be unreasonable. I hardly know her, we have just met, and...' Once again he was not allowed to say more.

'Oh, I should not let that deter you,' broke in his beloved bitterly. 'You obviously make a habit of hugging strange females in secluded places. Well, you may continue to do so, for all I care. I am sure I am very happy to have seen you in your true light. As for this—lady—I can only hope that she is more complaisant than I, for your sake. Come, Harry, we will leave this gentleman and his—friend—to themselves.' She turned away and Amanda, blushing vividly, hastened after her. Harry, not knowing what to do and feeling himself very much out of depth, gave a small shrug and went with them.

Robert stifled a groan, and looked down once again at his companion. Taken up with their reminiscences, he and Barney had walked much further than they had realised, and had quite failed to notice that the youthful bride had become very quiet, and remarkably pale. It was not until she had stumbled and almost fallen that Barney realised that his wife was far from well.

'Sally! What is it?' His alarmed tones made her rally, and she gave a sickly smile.

'Don't fret, Barney. I just feel faint, and—and a bit sick.' The effort of talking was too much, and she closed her eyes, leaning more heavily into their support as she felt her knees buckle under her.

'We must get help! A doctor! I will fetch a doctor at once!' Robert had never seen Barney in such a state.

'I fancy that would take some time, since we are in the middle of the Park. You would do better, Barney, to get your wife carried home as fast as may be. I know little of such matters, but I think such spasms are not unusual, in your wife's condition.'

'Oh, yes, just take me home,' whispered poor Sally, concentrating all her energies on subduing the rising nausea that threatened to overwhelm her. 'I should be all right directly, if only I could lie down.'

'Go and look for a cab, Barney, as quickly as may be!' Robert could see that his friend was still dithering, and thought it best to keep him occupied. From his own experience he knew how little help it was to be fussed over when unwell. 'You may call in the doctor as soon as you are at home, you know,' he added kindly, and was pleased to see his friend run off. Still supporting the invalid with a firm arm, he addressed her gently.

'There are no seats, so you cannot sit down, but let me take your weight, Mrs Ashstead, and try to breathe slowly and deeply.' Obediently she did as he said, and he had the satisfaction of seeing a tinge of colour return to her cheeks. It was at this moment that he heard footsteps on the path, and looking up beheld Harriet.

At the sound of her angry tones his companion shuddered, and turned very pale once more. He was so taken aback by Harriet's attack that he was unable to make her understand the circumstances of the case. Knowing that she was, in any case, overwrought by the discovery of his deception he cursed the chance that brought them together in this fashion. As Harriet turned the corner out of his sight he called her name, once, knowing as he did so that it was useless. If he could have run after her, made her listen to him, all might have been well, but he could not leave his friend's wife, whose weight still hung on his arm.

'I am so sorry to have made so much trouble,' she whispered.

He tried to put Harriet out of his mind, since there was nothing he could do, and concentrated on soothing his companion. 'It is nothing, the merest misunderstanding. You must not allow it to distress you.'

She gave the ghost of a smile. 'Was it, perhaps, a lover's quarrel?' she asked slyly.

Pleased to divert her mind, he admitted that it was.

'Then I do hope she will forgive you, when she understands the circumstances. She must care for you, or she wouldn't have been so angry,' she said wisely.

'Do you think you can walk a little, if we go very slowly? I think Barney will have found a cab by now, and he will be anxious to get you home, and call out half a dozen doctors.' He led her along the path towards the road, and within a few minutes Barney came running back to them. He would have carried his wife to the cab, but she persuaded him that it would attract too much attention, so he contented himself with holding her arm.

Once in the cab, she held out her hand to Robert with a shy smile. 'Thank you so very much for your help and your kindness, Sir Robert. I am sorry to have been so silly, and to have spoiled our first meeting. Do, pray, go now, and look for your friends.' She said no more in front of Barney, but gave him a speaking look.

Robert bowed over her hand. 'I shall do that. May I come and visit you soon, to see how you go on?'

'Yes, but do not delay. You might still be in time!'

Ignoring Barney's questions, Robert took her advice and hurried off.

Harriet would have hurried straight back to Grosvenor Square, but the children were not to be found, and it took several minutes of calling and scolding to gather them all together. They were hot and dusty. John had torn a hole in the knee of his trousers, and Augusta, not to be outdone, had ripped the skirt of her frock. Amanda did what she could with Harry's handkerchief to clean them up, and Harriet cobbled a hasty repair to the frock with pins from Amanda's reticule. The mundane activity gave time for her shock and anger to subside, and as her usual common sense returned she could have wept for shame at what she had said. That the young woman had been truly unwell she could not really doubt, and Amanda had ventured to whisper as much, pointing out that she had looked so very white. Why he should have been alone with her, as it seemed, in a secluded area of Kensington Gardens, was another matter.

While she did not really think him capable of making love to another girl so soon after declaring his love for her, she was still so shaken by the discovery of his deception that she was at a loss to know what to think. In the country everything had seemed so easy. She had felt sure of his love and of her own, and had felt that somehow, some day, they would be together and happy. Now it was as if the ground had turned to quicksand beneath her feet. Robert was not the man she had thought him, and she did not know him at all. Her heart told her to trust in his love, but she could not.

They were just leaving the Park when Robert caught up with them. He had seen them in the distance and run to catch them before they disappeared. Out of breath, he caught at her arm to stop her, and she turned angrily.

'Let go of me! How dare you!'

'For goodness' sake, Harriet, don't be so melodramatic! You surely cannot really think I was interested in that girl. She is married to one of my oldest friends, and is expecting a happy event. Her husband ran to fetch a cab when she felt faint, and I could hardly refuse to offer my help.'

'It means nothing to me,' said Harriet untruthfully.

'If that is so, I wonder why you made such an unmannerly fuss,' he said bluntly, stung into irritation.

He was right, and she knew it, which did nothing to mend her temper. She turned away from him. 'If I am so unmannerly, you had better have nothing more to do with me,' she said bitterly.

He was conscious of a strong desire to box her ears, and an equally strong desire to take her forcibly into his arms and kiss away her angry words and her frowns. Positioned as he was in the middle of an interested circle of her brothers and sisters, only the older of whom were even pretending not to listen, he could do neither. He lowered his voice and tried again. 'Harriet, I do not want to quarrel with you. Will you not listen to me? We have so much to discuss.'

'We have nothing to discuss.' Her words were cold but her voice was softer. He ventured to take her hand, and she did not withdraw it.

'Dearest Harriet, I cannot talk to you here. Only let me call on you again, and talk to you. You must believe that I never meant to hurt you by anything I did.' Her hand trembled in his, but at that moment the stentorian tones of Mrs Abbotsleigh rang out.

'Well, I thought her sadly fast on the night of her ball. She refused to dance with my cousin's son, to dance with that man, but holding hands in the Park! I would never allow any daughter of mine to behave in such a hoydenish way. And unchaperoned, too, for you cannot count the children, and her brother is wild to a fault, I hear, and up to his ears in debt. No doubt he has been sent down. Of course, she is after his money, for the Milbornes are as poor as church mice, and some people will go to any lengths...'

Scarlet with rage and embarrassment Harriet dragged her hand out of Robert's. He was too staggered by the vitriolic attack to prevent her, and Amanda was only just in time to prevent Harry from rounding on Mrs Abbotsleigh and giving her his opinion in a few pithy sentences.

'You see? You see what people are saying? Oh, it is too bad! You have made me the laughing stock of London. I never want to speak to you again!' Taking her brother's arm, she almost dragged him out of the park, and in a moment was out of sight in the traffic. Cursing all women, Robert returned to his lodgings.

CHAPTER FOURTEEN

AS THE DAYS passed, her family's hopes that Harriet would relent were proved to be unfounded. She refused even to speak his name. With a self-control that surprised them all she resumed her former round of gaieties, hiding her misery under a smiling face. If she lacked sparkle, she had more dignity, and Lady Cornelia even began to hope that some other eligible might take her interest. Only Amanda knew how many tears were shed at night, when there was no one to see.

Harry, meanwhile, was finding things difficult. At first in the excitement of his sister's affairs he was able to put his own troubles out of his mind, but now that things had settled down he saw that he could not prolong his absence from Oxford any longer, without running the risk of being sent down altogether. Returning to Oxford meant returning to Annie, or rather to her father, since it was he who was causing all the trouble.

His flight to London had solved nothing. Indeed, he had not really hoped that it would: he simply obeyed the age-old instinct to fly from danger. Unable to bring himself to confide in his father, he hesitated to talk to anyone else. He knew how easily society would pick up any hint of scandal in a noble family, and with what relish it would be discussed if it were to become known that the Earl of Pontesford's heir was about to be sued for breach of promise.

But what was he to do? Marriage was out of the question. While he had been, and still was, dazzled by Annie's delicate gold and white beauty, never for one moment could he have considered her as a life-time companion. He felt fairly sure that the offer of a substantial sum of money would lead to proceedings being dropped, but he had no such sum, nor could he see any way of raising it. His father, he knew, was already stretching his resources to the utmost to give Harriet her come-out. When, at Christmas, he had been forced to ask his father for money to pay his debts, he had found his parent surprisingly understanding. To be sure, he had scolded, but afterwards had spoken to his son man to man, showing him how the estate finances were arranged. Harry had been flattered to be treated as an adult, and had willingly given his word to curb his expenditure hereafter. This he had conscientiously done, and the Earl had been pleased. To ask him now for a sum of money to raise which it would be necessary to sell land, was a thing he could not do.

He wondered how little Annie's father would accept to solace her broken heart. Unfortunately, as the heir to a title, if not a fortune, he knew that her heart would not heal for the sort of amount that he, by selling everything valuable he possessed, and borrowing up to his limit, could raise.

He returned to Oxford in some gloom. Harriet, on bidding him farewell, had squeezed his hand meaningfully, and whispered that he was not to worry, she would do whatever she could to help. This promise filled him with dire forebodings, which he would have known were amply justified had he been able to see his sister, later in the same day, sitting at the little writing desk in her room and chewing thoughtfully at the end of her pen, in the throes of composing a letter.

As a distraction from her own misery, and overflowing with sympathy engendered by it for one whom she saw as deeply wronged, Harriet was determined on a course of action that would have horrified her family, had they known of it, but which was to make Annie's father rub his hands with delight. Having skilfully abstracted from the unconscious Harry Annie's name, place of work, and address, Harriet had decided to write to her. She would have preferred to have gone to Oxford herself, of course, to offer her support and comfort in person, but she found herself quite unable to think of any way in which this might be done. A letter was the next best thing. She wrote:

My dear Annie,
You will forgive me for addressing you thus informally, but since we are, I hope, to be Sisters one day, I cannot bring myself to call you Miss Chorlton. You will see from the above that my brother has told me All. I must assure you of my deep sympathy and concern. I am sure that Harry now sees that he is honour bound to make you his happy Bride. I am sure that my parents will soon learn to love you, and you can be assured that I shall do everything in my power to bring about that Happy Event which will unite you in happiness.

She frowned, feeling that the final phrase could have been better expressed. Reassuring herself that Annie, who was after all a shop girl, would scarcely bother herself over the niceties of self-expression, she let it stand, and moved to the conclusion.

I look forward with joy to meeting you one day soon. If, meanwhile, you would care to write to me, you

may do so by addressing the letter to my maid, Sarah
James. I know you will regret having to use this sub-
terfuge as much as I do, but my parents are as yet in
ignorance of our plans. I remain, my dear Annie,
your friend and sister-to-be,

Harriet Milborne.

It afforded her much satisfaction to send this artless
missive off to Oxford, where it was received with surprise
by Annie, who in Harry's absence had rather lost interest
in him, and with delight by her father, who saw in it a
powerful weapon. The poems were well enough in their
way, but did not in fact say anything very direct, whereas
with this, written and signed by the Viscount's sister and
speaking of his marriage as an assured thing, he might
even double his price! If the amount of joy we give to others be recorded in heaven, then surely Harriet's name was
written in gold that night!

After a few days a reply came, written under protest by
Annie on her father's orders. Harriet had to confess to
herself that she was rather disappointed with it. Annie's
handwriting was unformed and childish, her spelling indifferent, and the sentiments of gratitude she expressed
sounded somehow sycophantic. Her image of Annie as a
beautiful, innocent young girl wavered a little, but she
sternly repressed the feeling, reminding herself that one
should not judge anyone's heart by their spelling or their
handwriting, and that Annie was probably not very accustomed to expressing herself on paper.

The thought made her wonder how it would have been
had Robert written her such a letter. Of course, she now
knew that he had had the education of a gentleman, and
would write and spell as one. But if he had, in very truth,
been the Mr Roberts he had claimed to be, and had writ-

ten her in just such a way, would she have minded? She told herself ruefully that in him the mis-spellings would have been endearing, and she would have cherished every ill-formed letter. She could only hope that Harry would feel the same. It did not occur to her that had Robert been educated as Annie had been, she would have been unlikely to fall in love with him in the first place, for there would have been so little point of contact between their minds.

Harry was very worried. It had taken a great deal of fast talking to explain his absence in London. One night, to attend his sister's come-out ball, was one thing, but to continue to stay for a further three days quite another. Unable to explain his reasons, Harry was forced to divulge that there were family problems, whose nature he was not at liberty to discuss. Fortunately his genuinely worried face and manner lent substance to his claims, and he was let off with a warning. He returned to his rooms, where he found a letter, its threats only thinly veiled under a polite exterior, from Annie's father. He could have wept with despair.

The following day he stiffened himself for battle and went to Annie's home. It was evening, so he knew she would not be at work. A small hope that he might be able to see her alone, and persuade her to release him from whatever promise he was supposed to have made, was dashed by the sight of her father, his face wreathed in smiles, firmly placed on the rug in front of the empty fireplace.

'My lord! What a pleasure to see you! Here's my little Annie been quite pining away for you. Not a sight nor a word for all these days, and she breaking her heart all the while! "Oh, Pa," she says to me, "if he has deserted me, I know not how I shall go on living!" But I said to her,

"Don't you worry, my pet, his lordship's a gentleman, and the last thing any gentleman wants is a scandal in the family," I said. And here you are!' he finished triumphantly.

Harry looked at Annie, who showed few signs of pining away, for her shapely form was as well rounded as ever, and her cheeks flushed a delicate pink. On hearing her father's words, however, she obediently raised a lacy handkerchief to her eyes, and allowed a small sigh to escape her.

Harry tried to ignore Mr Chorlton, and spoke directly to Annie.

'Annie, do you really want to do this to me? I am sure, when we used to meet, that it was all innocent enough, and nothing was ever said or done to raise any expectations in you. Isn't that true? I know you liked me well enough, but you were always laughing and calling me a silly boy, and you never seemed interested in marrying me before.'

'No,' said Annie, 'but you see, I did not at first understand that you were a viscount, or that you will be an earl one day. I should like to be a countess,' she added simply, looking up at him with her large blue eyes.

'You would not like it, you know,' he said gently enough. 'My parents would be very angry, and would most probably cut off my allowance. We should be very poor, for I have no money of my own. I do not know how we should live. You would be a Lady, of course, but I am afraid we should both have to work hard.'

Mr Chorlton shook one finger waggishly at Harry. 'Shame on you, my lord, to mislead an innocent girl like that! She does not understand these things, of course, but you cannot tell me that the estate is not entailed with the title? When your esteemed father dies—and we all hope that day may be far distant—' he added piously, 'you are bound to inherit at least the land, and the house, whatever else may be left elsewhere.'

The worried look left Annie's face at her father's words. 'I should not mind being poor for a few years, if I knew we should have the big house some day. I should like it of all things, to live there, and have a lot of parties.'

'In any case, my lord,' the hatefully smooth voice continued, 'I cannot really believe that your esteemed parents, however angry they might be at the time, would allow you to starve! The Earl—a model parent, I am sure— would scarcely care for it to become known that his heir was reduced to working for a living, while his wife toiled as a skivvy! A quiet life abroad, perhaps...'

'Paris! I have always wanted to see Paris!'

Harry ground his teeth, and wondered why he had ever thought her so lovely. He did not believe there was any malice in her, she was simply being led by her father. He tried again. 'I cannot think, sir,' he said, turning to Mr Chorlton at last, 'that you would wish your daughter to enter into a loveless marriage with a man who has no money but what his parents choose to allow him, for the sake of a title and a future estate.'

Mr Chorlton threw up his hands. '*I* wish it? My dear Lord St Erth, I merely represent to you the feelings of my beloved daughter. It cannot be called a loveless marriage, for I am sure she is madly in love with you, and it is not so long since you professed a boundless love for her.'

'Did I say that?' Harry was appalled.

'Indeed you did, my lord. In those beautiful poems that I see poor Annie so often reading, with the tears falling down her face. Of course, the last thing I should wish to do is to cause any trouble, but I do wonder if the best thing might not be to send the poems to your honoured father, and have his opinion. I am sure he would not wish his son to behave dishonourably.'

'You scoundrel, do not dare to address my father!'

Chorlton's smile merely widened. 'My lord, calm your-self. I said I did not want to make any trouble. But my daughter, my lord, my only chick, my motherless child, she is all I have. And I must do the best I can for her, must I not? Such is the precious duty of parenthood, as you will learn one day, my lord, in the fullness of time.'

'I will never marry her. I would rather cut my throat!'

'That would certainly break your parents' hearts, and cause a scandal, but I dare say you would not care for that, by then. Think it over, my lord, I beg you, and do not be too hasty.'

'There is nothing to think over. I will not marry her.'

'Then you must compensate her for her bitter disap-pointment.' The steel was showing now, and Harry was almost relieved.

'And just how much money would it take to heal her heart? How much am I worth, on the open market?'

Mr Chorlton named a sum that made Harry reel in-wardly, though he did his best to remain impassive. He was shrewd enough to know that his opponent had over-stated his case, and would probably be prepared to accept a lower figure than the one named, but even half the sum would represent a severe loss to his father, should it have to be paid. Land must be sold, probably Amanda's come-out postponed for another year, and all for the sake of a few trumpery poems.

'I will consider your offer,' he said through gritted teeth, and slammed from the house, leaving Chorlton looking pleased with himself.

'I think we have him on the run, my dear,' he said hap-pily. 'That is a very worried young man.'

'I really don't think I want to marry him, if he is going to be so disagreeable,' offered Annie. 'I'm sure he's not nearly as nice as young Mr Stockleigh I met the other day.'

'Be quiet, my dear. Of course you need not marry him. He said himself, he has no fortune at all. But his father could raise it, if he wanted. And I fancy he will want, to keep his heir out of trouble. I must think about it. Give me the poems, girl, and let me have another look at them. I might want to write to the Earl.'

'Oh dear, Pa, I am not sure where I put them,' said Annie calmly. 'I had them yesterday, or was it the day before? And then we had a visitor, and I laid them down— now where did I put them? I hope they haven't been thrown away.'

Her loving parent boxed the ears of his motherless chick, and adjured her to find the papers forthwith. It was as well for her that he did not know their true fate. In a moment of abstraction she had torn them up, and used them for curl papers. They were just the right degree of stiffness.

CHAPTER FIFTEEN

ROBERT REMAINED in London. His first instinct had been to return at once to Atherington Hall, and bury himself in work. After a night's sleep, however, he knew that he must remain. He could not believe that Harriet could cast out the love he felt sure she felt for him. He thought that Sally Ashstead had been right, when she said that Harriet would not have been so angry with him in the park had she not still cared for him. He had wanted the chance to see her again, and had had it, and things were now worse than ever. Yet he was still convinced that a quiet, rational conversation would put everything to rights.

He called at the house in Grosvenor Square, but Harriet refused to be at home to him. The butler denied her with regret. Lady Cornelia, the Earl, Amanda, all of them begged her to see him, but Harriet shut herself in her room and threatened to take to her bed for a month if she were forced downstairs. Deep down she knew that her defences were not proof against him, that he had only to take her into his arms and kiss her to make her forget, at least for a while, all her anger. She wanted it to be so, yet she would not fail to keep faith with her own feeling of what was right.

Robert called a second and a third time. 'I regret, sir, that Lady Harriet is not at home to visitors,' he was told once again.

'Not at home to *me*, you mean,' he muttered. To his amazement the impassive face creased with sympathy, the butler's distant air banished by a look of fatherly concern.

'My advice, sir, is don't give up,' he said confidentially. 'It's a good sign.'

'What is? That she won't see me?'

'Yes, sir. Now, if she felt really sure of what she was doing, she'd see you soon enough, and tell you to your face, too. Trust me, sir, I know what I'm talking about.'

Robert was amused, and touched at his concern. 'You have been a long time with the family, I suppose?'

'Oh, yes, sir. Started as under-footman, more than twenty years ago. Why, I remember Lady Harriet being born. Early, she was, and such a fuss as you never did see. And yell—the nurse said she'd never any fear of her surviving, though she was so tiny. A fighter, that's what she is, sir. In the best way, of course, if you know what I mean.'

Rather comforted, Robert took the butler's advice and continued to call regularly, refusing to be daunted by her denials. He and the butler came to be on remarkably good terms, and Robert was able to keep abreast with everything his love was doing. He knew when she was to go to the play, or a ball, and when she (rarely) had an evening at home. His sense of honour was too nice to permit him to use this information to dog her footsteps, though he sometimes took up a post behind a pillar in the Opera House or theatre when he knew she was to be there, so as to get a sight of her. He laughed at himself as he did so, feeling that he was behaving no better than a lovesick adolescent, but he could not forgo the pleasure of an occasional glimpse. It seemed to him that she was looking paler than of wont, and that, too, encouraged him to continue hoping.

Then came just such a chance as he had been praying for. A friend from the Crimea, Charles Dulverston, invited him to a small private dance which he and his wife were holding. Robert knew that the Milbornes were acquainted with him, through their friendship with the Marquis and Marchioness of Berrington. Presuming on their friendship, he begged Emily Dulverston to send an invitation to the Milbornes. He had only met her since his arrival in London, though she had married his friend three years earlier, but had found her delightfully sympathetic, for she herself was not a stranger to the problems of courtship.

'There was a time when I thought I should not be able to marry my dear Charles,' she confided, 'so I know just how you feel. I am sure it will all come right in the end.'

He took care not to arrive too early at the dance, for he did not want to be there before Harriet arrived. When he finally entered the room he gave Mrs Dulverston a perfunctory greeting, while anxiously searching among the dancing couples.

'She is over there, dancing with Lord Istead,' said his hostess kindly. Robert looked, and their eyes met. There was a flash of joy on her face, and then an instant rejection. The movement of the dance carried her away, but not before he had seen the stony look she wore.

During the next hour he danced conscientiously with the plainest girls he could find, so as to give his beloved no more ammunition. She, for her part, was bent on showing him how much she was enjoying herself, talking, laughing and dancing with such vivacity that the little group around her was in danger of degenerating into a romp. Waiting for his moment, he did not attempt to approach her, when he became aware that she was nowhere to be seen. With a muttered apology to his partner he left her at the end of the dance, and went in search of Harriet.

He did not need to look very far. There was a small sitting room not far away. Harriet, while dancing once again with Lord Istead, had had her skirt torn by a clumsy step by her partner, and had withdrawn to effect a temporary repair. Lord Istead, who was very young and, it is to be regretted, rather drunk, had no sooner found himself alone with her than he had attempted to take her into his arms. She, well aware of his condition and unwilling to create a scene, was attempting to fend off his inept embraces when Robert strode in.

One glance was enough. He strode forward and took the youthful lord by the scruff of his neck, and with one swift jerk pulled him away from Harriet. The champagne was still fizzing in the young man's blood.

'How dare you in-intrude between me and the woman I love?' he stammered, swinging a wild fist that Robert had no difficulty in evading.

'How dare you press your unwelcome attentions on this lady?' replied Robert grimly. 'Go and stick your head under the pump, you young puppy.'

Lord Istead, muzzily aware that his assailant was considerably larger, older and probably wiser than he, looked suddenly like the puppy he had been called, and left the room shamefaced. Robert turned to Harriet.

'That was cruel. He meant no harm.'

'Come, Harriet, you surely did not want him to kiss you, did you?'

She was mortified at having been found in so uncomfortable a situation, above all by him. 'Whether I did or not, it is nothing to do with you at all events,' she snapped, her cheeks crimson with embarrassment and rage.

'I would have done the same for any young lady.'

'But I am not any young lady! Oh, why did it have to be you? Why can't you leave me alone?' Scarcely knowing what she did or said, she ran from the room. Robert waited for a few moments, not wishing for them to be seen coming from so secluded a place together, but by the time he returned to the dance Harriet had gone home.

In desperation, he wrote a long letter to Lady Beatrice. He told her everything, trusting her to judge the rights and wrongs of the case. He was surprised when she did not write back. She was in general, as he knew from experience, an indefatigable correspondent, and could be relied on to reply to any letter, however trivial, as quickly as possible. He hoped that she was not ill, then reassured himself that if that were the case he would surely have been told. He was surprised, but gratified, when a few days later there was an imperious knocking at the door of his lodgings, and a few moments later Barton announced Lady Beatrice herself.

He leaped to his feet. 'My dear aunt! Here is a pleasant surprise. I had no idea you were coming to town. Where are you putting up? I would have come to see you at once, if you had sent, and saved you the effort of coming here.'

'Came at once,' said Lady Beatrice telegraphically, panting slightly from the effort of climbing his stairs. 'Had to talk to you. More private here. No privacy in hotels, even good ones. Never know who might be listening.'

'Sit down, aunt, and rest before you talk. Barton! Something for her ladyship! Will you have tea, or madeira? I would not for the world have had you make all this effort on my behalf.'

'I'll take some madeira, thank you. Tea's too insipid at this time of day, and I won't deny I need something after those stairs.' Lady Beatrice subsided thankfully into a

chair, and sipped gratefully at the glass of madeira that
Barton was quick to bring her. 'Barton, isn't it? My
nephew has told me about you, and I believe I have to
thank you for your care of him when he was wounded.'

Barton looked horribly embarrassed, and muttered
something indistinguishable about duty and pleasure.

'Now, Barton, I must have a good talk to your master.
Do make sure we are not disturbed.' Barton bowed and left
the room. 'Now then, Robert, whatever have you been
about? You find yourself a perfectly acceptable girl, the
sort of girl you told me did not exist, and now I hear that
she'll have none of you, though from what you said at first
I understood that all was more or less arranged between
you.'

'I am afraid I have made a great muddle of it, aunt.'

'Now that's no way to be talking! I own I couldn't see
the reason for all these charades and assumed names, but
you didn't set out to deceive the girl on purpose. If you ask
me, you've been too soft with her. She tells you how
wicked and deceitful you are, and what do you do? Agree
with her!'

'But I did behave badly, aunt. I should have told her the
truth from the very first.'

'There you go again! That's no way to behave with a
young girl. If you agree with her, and tell her that you have
behaved wrongly, and so on, what can she do? She can
hardly back down and say that it doesn't matter.'

'I am not a cave-man, aunt. I cannot abduct her forcibly. She will not even speak to me.'

'She cannot prevent you from speaking to her.'

'I could not force her to listen to me in so public a place.'

'All the better. She could not refuse to hear you, without making a public scene.'

He smiled. 'You do not know my Harriet, aunt! She might just do that very thing! Do you think I want to bring the gossips gathering round her like vultures?'

'There is such a thing,' she said darkly, 'as being too generous. I can see that I shall have to speak to her myself.'

Robert did not know whether to be glad or worried. 'She may refuse to see you too, aunt.'

'She will scarcely be able to if I am staying in the same house,' returned his great-aunt triumphantly. 'I arrived only last night, and put up at an hotel, which I detest doing. Now I shall ask my god-daughter Cornelia to have me to stay for a few days.'

'Will she do so?'

'She will not like to refuse. Very correct, Lady Cornelia. She always does the right thing. She wouldn't turn a poor old woman from her door.'

Robert burst out laughing. 'You are up to every trick in the book, Aunt Beatrice. With you on my side, I do not see how I can lose!'

'We shall see. Now you shall take me back to my hotel, and I shall write a note to Cornelia. You may expect to hear from me in a day or two.'

Lady Cornelia was far from pleased to receive her godmother's letter. 'Really, as if we hadn't more than enough troubles already,' she complained to the Earl. 'She is Sir Robert's great-aunt, too, so it is quite obvious why she has come to London at this juncture, for I am sure she has not been near us for years. Now we shall have Harriet being rude to her, and I don't know what else, and I shall go distracted!'

'Harriet has very good manners, my dear. I am sure you have seen to that.'

'Oh, she won't intend to be rude, but you know what she is...sometimes she says the first thing that comes into her head, and if she is upset... I must have a talk to her, and implore her not to upset things any more than she has already done.'

'Can't you tell the old girl that we have no room?'

'I couldn't do that, Henry. She is my god-mother, after all. Besides, it isn't true, and you can be sure she knows just how many rooms we have here.'

'Maybe she will be able to get Harriet to see reason.'

'Maybe she will. But I don't hold out much hope.'

On this dispiriting note Lady Cornelia departed to write a suitably welcoming note to her unwanted guest, and to give orders to have her room prepared.

Fortune, however, smiled on Lady Cornelia. Lady Beatrice, arriving that afternoon with her maid and what seemed like a mountain of baggage, admitted to feeling very tired after her journey from Bath, and retired straight away to rest. She did not emerge for some hours, and when she did found that Harriet was engaged for the entire evening, dining with friends and afterwards attending a party under the protection of her friend's mother, an old acquaintance of the family.

'I was sure you would not mind if Harriet kept to her evening's engagements, although you have just arrived, Lady Beatrice,' said the Countess gracefully. 'She was so sorry not to have seen you, and looks forward to making your acquaintance tomorrow.' She offered up a swift prayer for forgiveness for thus altering the truth. Harriet had in fact said, 'I can't face meeting her, Mama! Must I see her?'

Lady Beatrice was sorry, but was still feeling more than usually tired. During the evening she sneezed several times, and at length was brought to admit that her throat was sore, and her head throbbing. Lady Cornelia was concerned.

'I am afraid you have caught cold on your journey, Godmother. May I ring for something for you? I have some very effective pastilles.'

'Thank you, no. My maid will know what to do for me. I think I will say goodnight, and retire early.'

With some relief, for she had feared she was to have spent an evening being forced to discuss Harriet's behaviour, Lady Cornelia saw her guest to her room, made sure that she had everything that she needed, and withdrew to spend an unaccustomed quiet evening with the Earl and Amanda. The next morning Harriet awoke to the news that Lady Beatrice had succumbed to a heavy cold, and was keeping to her bed.

'Oh, good! At least, I mean I am very sorry for her, and I hope she will soon be better. It is not serious, is it, Mama?'

'I think not, though I have offered to call the doctor, for at her age, you know, one must take every care. It seems she never feels completely well away from Bath, though I cannot imagine why. So very old-fashioned, and that nasty water—ugh! Anyway, I have said that you must on no account see her until she is over the worst. She quite understands that we cannot have you taking her cold now, in the middle of your season.'

'Thank you, Mama. I am sorry to be causing all this trouble.'

'I must say, I had not expected it of you, Harriet. That is to say, I feared there might be some—difficulties—but I did not think it would be like this!' Perceiving that there were tears in her daughter's eyes, she added hastily, 'Still, we won't talk of it now. Make haste and get up, for I wish you to come shopping with me.'

Harriet obediently allowed her maid to dress her in a very becoming walking dress of primrose silk faille, with a matching jacket fitting close to her body, and sleeves of the new, wider shape. It was the first time she had worn it, and as she tied the neat bonnet trimmed with a frill of lace and rosettes of primrose ribbons over her smoothly banded hair, she found herself absent-mindedly wishing that Robert could see her. She banished the thought, and went sadly downstairs.

Robert was disappointed that morning to receive a short note from his great-aunt telling him of her indisposition. She assured him that it would not be of long duration, and that she would be speaking to Harriet very soon, but he went off to his club in a very ill humour, where he lost some money at backgammon, and drank rather too much wine. He determined that he was not going to waste very much more time. If Lady Beatrice did not manage to see Harriet in the next few days, he would confront her one evening when she was out, and demand that she give him one more interview. If that failed, he would leave London.

CHAPTER SIXTEEN

MR CHORLTON, that devoted father, was much exercised in his mind. He had been extremely angry with his daughter when she had confessed that she could no longer find the Viscount's poems. (She had not been able to bring herself to tell him what had become of them.) His dismay, as he saw a small fortune disappearing rapidly over the horizon, was great, but was allayed only two days later by the arrival of Harriet's letter.

Here were riches indeed. What were the poems compared to this? Chorlton was well aware that if he tried to sue the Viscount for breach of promise he had nothing to gain, since that innocent young gentleman was under-age. For the same reason Chorlton did not want to drive the young man too hard—one visit to the family lawyer would soon put paid to his schemes. No, his best bet was to hold the threat of discovery over the young man's head. The poems, had they still existed, might have been used to show to the Earl, but Chorlton was well aware that an older man, while he might be willing to pay to have the poems back, would not have been likely to pay a great deal. As a last resort, a hint to the newspapers that a small insertion along the lines that the Viscount St E—, eldest son of the Earl of P—, was romantically attached to Miss A—C—of Messrs G—and R—, Outfitters, of Oxford, would be almost certain to do the trick.

Meanwhile, the letter fell into his hand like a shower of gold from heaven, and he must use it to the best advantage. They had not seen or heard from Harry since his last visit several days before. That young gentleman, at his wits' end, had decided to imitate the action of the ostrich and bury his head, in lieu of sand, in his work. He studied so hard that his friends were concerned, and his tutor prided himself that his stern words and admonitions had at last borne fruit. Harry, like Mr Micawber, hoped devoutly that something would turn up, and had a confused sort of idea that if he did well in his studies he would in some way be earning merit to galvanise some guardian angel into activity.

Mr Chorlton read through the letter for the tenth time, and came to a decision. He sought out his daughter, who was re-trimming a bonnet with scraps of silk brought home from her place of work. 'My dear,' he said pontifically, 'I have made up my mind. We shall go to London.'

Miss Annie Chorlton, startled but not displeased, looked up from her work. 'Lord, Pa, whatever for?' she inquired.

'Do not trouble your pretty head about it,' he said grandly. 'Let it be enough for you that I have A Plan.'

She was used to his attitudes, and not inclined to be impressed.

'Really, Pa, I *must* trouble my pretty head about it. When are we to go, for one thing, and for how long? I've my job to consider. They won't be best pleased if I go off just like that. I've the chance of being put up to cravats and gloves when Miss Smith goes, and I don't want to miss that.'

'Cravats and gloves! To think that a daughter of mine should demean herself...'

'Well, Pa, you were pleased enough when I took on the job,' she pointed out.

'That was then. Now is quite a different matter.' he said with incontrovertible truth. 'My child, if My Plan should work, you would never need to enter the doors of that shop again.'

'You mean I'll be a Lady? I thought you said I wasn't going to have to marry him.'

'I mean, my child, that we shall be rich. Rich enough, at any rate, to leave this miserable house. In fact, we might leave Oxford altogether.'

'But I like Oxford. I don't want to leave, Pa. There's all the young men, and a girl can have plenty of fun here. I don't see that there's so much wrong with this house either. It's always been good enough for us before, and it was good enough for Ma, too.'

'My dear, the world is full of young men, and while this house may have been good enough for us once, it will scarcely do for ever. Your dear Ma, may she rest in peace, would have been the first to say the same. Such plans as she had for you! Let me see, how old are you now?'

'Seventeen. Really, Pa!'

'Seventeen? I had thought you were only sixteen, but no matter. You have many years ahead of you, before your beauty begins to fade. We can travel, my child. A whole world of possibilities is opening out before us.'

'I don't know what you're going on about,' said Annie crossly. 'My beauty fade? I hope I shall be married, and settled down, long before I need to worry about that.'

'And so do I, dear girl, so do I. But not, I beg of you, too soon. Think of it—a year here, a year there, the young men, the gifts, the poems...'

'I hope you're not suggesting what I think you might be,' said his dear child mutinously, 'because if you are, you can put it right out of your head. I'm a good girl, and I mean to stay that way.'

Mr Chorlton was shocked. 'How could you let such a thought sully your mind, still less your lips and my ears,' he said severely. 'I meant no such thing. But as I said, the world is full of young men, rich and well born. Young men will fall for a pretty face, and many times they'll say things to a girl when they're in love that their parents might not be too pleased about. Or better still,' he added thoughtfully, 'write them.'

She thought for a few minutes, her fingers automatically pleating the rosette of silk she was fashioning. 'You mean, like this time, but keep on doing it? Go out looking for them, perhaps, instead of meeting by chance as I did Harry—his lordship, that is?'

'Why not?' he asked simply.

'I don't think I like the idea, somehow,' she said slowly. 'I wasn't all that happy about this time, only you would do it. You know I never meant it to happen. It was all by chance, and I knew very well he meant nothing by those silly poems. I don't think I could do it again, not in cold blood. I'm not sure that I even want to do it now. He's done me no harm, and I don't like it. What's more, I don't think Ma would have liked it, either.'

'How can you be so undutiful?' he asked, then subdued his anger to reason with her. 'My love, do not think I do not understand your scruples. They do you great honour, and in fact I share them. But, I ask you, can we, poor as we are, afford to have such scruples? They are all very well for the rich, who never have to worry about how to live. But I am not getting any younger, and nor are you. Your pretty face, God bless you for it, is all we have. It is a gift. It would be wicked not to use it. Sinful, even.' She was unresponsive. He continued. 'If you had another gift, like singing, or dancing, would you not use it?'

'I suppose so. But it doesn't seem fair, somehow.'

'Fair? What's fair? Is it fair that some people are born never having to lift a finger, never having to work? You might as well say, is it fair to animals for us to eat them. We're all hunters, after a living. If we were gentlefolk, we'd go after grouse, or salmon, or partridge. As it is, we go after those who have what we want, and what we want is money. So we go after the rich.'

'I must say, Pa,' she said admiringly, 'you really can talk. You should be on the stage, or in a pulpit, or something.'

'I have often felt,' he admitted modestly, 'that my station in life has not allowed me to make full use of my undoubted talents. In a better world, my dear, I should probably have been Prime Minister. Or a Bishop. As it is, I'm just a poor man with one child, who refuses to lift a finger to help her old father, who's done the best for her all his life.' He sat down, and covered his eyes with one hand.

'Don't say that, Pa,' she cried, casting her bonnet aside. 'It's only that I don't want to be doing anything wrong.'

'Of course you don't, Annie. No more do I. You don't suppose I'd really take that young man to court, do you? I'd never do that, now.' It was an easy enough promise to make, since he knew well that a court case would do him no good at all. His daughter was mollified.

'All right, then, Pa. I'll come with you to London. But I make no promises for the future, mind. Now tell me, what are we going to do?'

'First thing in the morning, we'll send a message to the shop to say that you cannot come in, as your father needs you at home. Isn't that true enough, in a way? Then you and I, in our best clothes, take the train for London, and go to call on your friend.'

'My friend? Who might that be? I don't know a soul in London.'

'Do you not? What about your new friend, who has promised to help you? Your friend Lady Harriet Milborne?'

'Oh, Pa, whatever next? What am I to say to her? I've never talked to a real Lady before, not in her own house, and that. Suppose they won't let us in? There'll be a butler, and footmen, and all.'

'They'll let us in all right, don't you worry. And as for what you'll say, you can leave all that to me. In fact, I want you to. We don't want to go all that way for you to say the wrong thing.'

'Very good, Pa.'

'That's my girl! Now you go and look out your prettiest frock, for we want you to appear to advantage. Not too low cut, mind. Young and innocent, that's how I want you.'

'That's what I am, Pa,' said Annie indignantly.

'I know you are, but that's not to the purpose. The important thing is that they know you are, and how are they to know it if you don't show 'em? And an early night, mind.'

'Yes, Pa. Goodnight Pa.'

'Goodnight, girlie. Oh, and tell that girl to bring me some rum, and lemons. I'll make myself a bowl of punch. I've got plenty of thinking to do, this evening. Now off you go.'

Annie went obediently upstairs, and made her clothes ready for the morning. It was fortunate, she thought, that she had all but re-trimmed the bonnet. A few stitches, and it was done. She was both excited and nervous. Instinct, and a lifetime's knowledge of her father's ways, made her suspicious of his promises. Though she had been carried away at first by the thought of being a Countess, she was not fundamentally a dishonest girl, and her parent's schemes for preying on the rich, however plausibly presented, did not altogether appeal to her. It was true that she would like to have some money, enough so that she could leave her present place at the shop, and set up on her own. Millinery, she thought, looking admiringly at the refurbished bonnet, was something she had a flair for. With a little capital, enough to get her going, she was sure she could make a success of it. Also, unknown to Pa, she had noticed the under-manager of the shop eyeing her appreciatively on more than one occasion. He was a nice looking young man, she thought, not too young but not too old either. A good, steady sort, who would make (she blushed) a good husband and father.

That, however, was for the future. At present she was stuck with Pa, and his schemes. As she curled up her side hair, (using for the purpose the remains of the much disputed poems), she thought hard. She was fond of Harry, in a mild way. He was good company, and of course a Viscount, though whatever she had said to him she had never seriously considered him as a possible husband. In her eyes, young in years though she was, she was older in experience by far then he, and to her he seemed a mere boy. Nevertheless, she was unwilling to hurt him. Some money she would accept, because she needed it and however much he might plead poverty he was not in fact poor. But she would have no hand in ruining him.

Her hair neatly curled, she tied the strings of her nightcap becomingly under one ear, then fetched out a piece of paper, pen and ink, and addressed herself to writing, the tip of her tongue firmly clamped between her teeth. It was not a task that came easily to her, and necessitated much scratching out, and blotting, but in the end she was satisfied.

> My dear Harry,
> This is to warn you that Pa and me are off to London tomorrow, that is, today (Tuesday) [she added for further clarity, not knowing when he would be likely to get her missive] We are going to see your Sister who rote me such a lovely letter saying she would help me and all. But do not worry [heavily underlined, and with a spatter of ink at the end] as I will try not to let him do anything dredfull, and I beg to remane, Sir, your most obedient Annie.

This last she lifted without benefit of spelling from a business letter she had seen in the shop, and she felt it added a touch of formality and class.

Folding the note carefully, she crept down to the kitchen, where, as she expected, there was a sound of scuffling as she opened the door.

'It's all right, Tillie, it's only me,' she said to the maid-of-all-work. 'Who is it, the baker's boy?'

'Yes, miss. Sorry, miss,' muttered Tillie as she sheepishly drew that stalwart lad from behind the kitchen door, where he had been vainly attempting to hide. 'Only I do get so lonely down here, miss, all by myself of an evening.'

'Well, so long as it doesn't happen too often. As it happens for this once it suits me very well. Do you know Balliol College?' This to the lad, who was trying to be invisible.

'Yes, miss, course, miss,' he mumbled shyly, his eyes fixed on his boots, although Annie thought that in her cotton nightgown and wrap she was actually more decently covered than in the daytime.

She held out the note, which he took without raising his eyes. 'Take this to the porter at Balliol. I have written the direction on the outside. It is to be given to—to the person I am sending it to—as soon as possible. Is that quite clear?'

'Yes, miss, course, miss,' he repeated, still standing before the range and studying his boots.

'Well, get along with you, then,' she said crossly. 'Didn't you hear me say I wanted it there as soon as possible? And mind, not a word to anyone.'

'Yes, miss, course, miss.' On the third repetition he vanished into the night. Tillie locked the door virtuously, with the air of one performing a task she had been wanting to do for some time. Annie looked doubtfully at her.

'Will he manage it, do you think?'

'Oh, yes, miss. He's very reliable. Leastways, he nearly always brings the right bread.'

With this assurance, Annie had perforce to be satisfied.

CHAPTER SEVENTEEN

As LUCK would have it, Harry did not receive Annie's letter until later the following morning. The baker's boy had vindicated Tillie's trust in him by faithfully delivering it to the porter, who had handed it to the scout to be given to the Viscount. He, however, was not in his room. As has been mentioned, his sudden attack of studying had worried his friends. Heretofore a careless, though not unintelligent, scholar, he had thrown himself into his work with an abandon that they could not understand at all. After some days a small delegation arrived to see him, finding him pale, ink-stained and surrounded by half-finished books.

'Now then, St Erth, what is all this?' The leader of the group had led the attack. He had been at Eton with Harry, and knew him better than most.

'Clear off, you chaps,' growled their host ungraciously. 'Can't you see I'm busy?'

'Busy? You can't be busy all the time. Come on, Harry. You haven't any exams this year. I know we've been overdoing it a bit, one way and another, but killing yourself over your books won't put that to rights.'

'Mustn't disappoint my father,' muttered Harry. 'I promised him I'd keep out of debt, and I shall. Out of trouble, too.'

'Of course you shall! I'm not asking you to come to a card party—dash it all, man, it's only three o'clock in the afternoon! Just a bit of fun on the river, you know. Fresh air, and all that. You look as though you could do with it. If you ask me, your father would be the first one to say so.'

This was quite true. The Earl, not a bookish man himself, would have been horrified to see his heir shutting himself up over his books in this way.

'Who's going?' asked Harry, looking a little more interested. It was true that his brain was buzzing with the sudden influx of ill-digested studies, and the prospect of a couple of hours in a punt seemed very inviting, and harmless, too. A sudden suspicion struck him.

'What I mean is, is it just you three?'

'Of course. Did you want to invite anyone else?'

'No girls?'

His friend looked at him in sudden understanding. It had not escaped his notice that Harry had been seeing a certain amount of that pretty little blonde shop girl. He had not given it a thought—such things were not uncommon, and it was hardly his business. A suspicion that all might not be well crossed his mind, but he wisely held his tongue for the moment. 'No girls,' he promised soothingly. 'Just Westbrook, here, and Elverton, and myself. And you, if you'll come.'

'All right, I'll come,' Harry decided, jumping to his feet and feeling rather more cheerful.

'Capital! That's the spirit, old man. Bustle along, then, and change. Wash some of the ink off, too, if you can. We don't want to be seen with a swot!'

Harry enjoyed his afternoon, and succeeded for the most part in putting his troubles out of his mind. They took the punt up-river, exchanging insults with other passing craft, and criticising their friends' skill with happy insouciance. The afternoon was sunny and warm, punting was thirsty work. Pretty waterside inns were inviting, and numerous. The journey home was hilarious and erratic, all four arriving back at their colleges very damp, and rather the worse for wear. The combination of fresh air, sunshine, exercise and beer made Harry so sleepy that he hardly bothered to undress before he tumbled into bed and asleep. Annie's note, pushed under his door by the scout, lay hidden under his abandoned coat. Harry slept long and well.

Familiar with the ways of young gentlemen, his scout did not hurry to waken him in the morning. When Harry finally opened bleary eyes it was already ten o'clock, and his scout was picking up the abandoned clothes, shaking his head over the damp and mud, and picking disparagingly at a patch of duckweed encrusted on the shoulder of the coat. Harry sat up, ran a hand through tousled hair, then drank thirstily from the large cup of tea the scout had set beside him.

'That's better. Mouth like a sand-pit. Sorry about the clothes—I went out on the river yesterday. What's the time?'

'Close to ten o'clock, my lord.'

'Too late to worry about that lecture, then. Never make it by half past.' Not very worried, Harry leaned back against the pillows and held out his cup for a refill.

The scout resumed his previous task, and reaching the bottom of the heap of garments found the letter, still neatly folded, lying on the floor. He held it out to Harry. 'This arrived last evening, my lord. I put it under your door, as you were out.'

'Lord, I was far too drunk to be reading letters when I got in,' said Harry cheerfully. 'What is it, a bill?'

'I wouldn't like to say, my lord. The porter said it was delivered by hand, quite late.' Years of experience had taught the scout a great deal of discretion. It had not escaped his notice that the handwriting on the note was decidedly feminine, but it was not his place to be officially aware of such things.

'Pass it over, then.' Unsuspiciously Harry unfolded the piece of paper, and read the contents. Then he sat up, and read them again, more carefully.

'Good Lord,' he groaned. 'That's done it!' He leaped out of bed. 'I must get dressed at once, Baines. Not a moment to lose. Quick, man, my clothes!'

'Very good, my lord.' Baines was imperturbable. 'What clothes would you wish, my lord?'

'Oh, London clothes,' said Harry, beginning to shave a furious speed and cursing as he had to pause and strop his razor.

'Certainly, my lord. Nothing untoward, I trust?'

'So do I trust it, but I wouldn't like to bet any money on it,' replied the Viscount, dabbing at a welling spot of blood where he had cut himself. 'What time's the next train?'

'I believe there's one by half past ten, my lord.'

'I'll have to try and get that one, then,' said Harry, quite forgetting the previous impossibility of attending a lecture at just that time. He flung on his clothes, ran from college to station, and just threw himself into the train as it was about to pull out of the station.

Luckily for him his carriage was empty and he drew Annie's letter from the pocket into which he had thrust it before leaving, and read it for the third time. It did not seem to have become any less appalling with the passage of time. In fact, it made his blood run cold.

So Harriet had written to Annie! He remembered now, with rage, those artfully unconcerned questions, and how he had cheerfully divulged Annie's name and address. Fool that he was! And Harriet, not content with making a muddle of her own life, must now do the same with his! He had little faith in Annie's assurance that she would not let her father cause any trouble. The mere fact of their presence in Grosvenor Square would be trouble enough. Calling down curses on the heads of all females, and on himself if he ever had anything to do with them again, Harry endured the journey to London, which seemed to him to be taking several years.

Annie and her father were not so very far ahead of him. In spite of his intentions about an early start, an overindulgence of punch had made that gentleman, like Harry, sleep later than he had wished. Annie did not hurry to waken him, for she was busy with her toilette. A visit to London, and to such elevated company, required careful preparation. Tillie was made to heave and heave again on the stay-laces, until her waist, already small, reached the minuscule proportions that satisfied her. Petticoats followed, layer upon layer of them, for Annie had not yet managed to purchase one of the new hooped contraptions. She only hoped she would not die of heat on the train.

Next her hair, the back in a smooth knot, the front, newly released from its papers, falling in careful, sausage-shaped curls. No lady could have finer, she thought, admiring the golden shine of them as they bounced against her white skin.

The gown, her finest, was of sky-blue lustring. The thin fabric shimmered in the sunlight, and the full skirts were decked with bows, rosettes, and frills. It was perhaps more suitable to an evening party than a morning visit, but it was the best one she had. A smart jacket of deeper blue velvet, and the newly trimmed bonnet, completed the ensemble. Annie turned in front of the looking glass complacently.

'Oh, miss, you do look lovely,' breathed Tillie, quite overcome.

'I wouldn't want those smart London people thinking we're just dowdy country mice. Now then, Tillie, if we should be delayed tonight, you're to lock the house up properly, sharp on nine. And no callers, do you hear me?'

Her father's call sent her running down the stairs. He, too, looked approvingly at her. 'Very good. Sweetly pretty. Stay, undo your jacket. Yes, as I thought. Perhaps just a trifle low cut, my dear.'

'Oh, Pa, it's the fashion!'

'Remember what I said, my dear. Young, and innocent. Perhaps, a little draping of lace?' Annie returned to her room, and sulkily arranged a lace scarf across shoulders and breast.

'Much better,' he approved. 'Dear me, it is rather later than I had intended, but we shall still be in London by lunch time. Come, Annie.' With stately grace he offered her his arm, and in good spirits they set off to the station.

Harry, on reaching London, jumped from his train before it had stopped moving, and ran through the crowds to the street. Hailing a hansom, he leaped into it, adjuring the driver to go as fast as he liked to Grosvenor Square. What he was to do there when he arrived he did not know. A wild vision of waylaying Annie and her father in the street as they arrived was scarcely practical, especially as he had no way of knowing the time they would come. Indeed, for all he knew, they might already be there. He groaned.

'Can't you drive any faster?' he shouted to the driver.

'Not without I kill the 'orse, guv, and meself too,' came the response. 'We'll be there soon enough, don't you fret.'

A moment later the driver's prognostications seemed to be likely to come true. They were bowling at a smart trot along the Bayswater Road when an over-laden cart, full of furniture, lumbered out from Albion Street. The driver, distracted for a moment as he turned to speak to Harry, was on top of it before he was aware. A fierce pull on the traces succeeded in turning the horse, but the sudden movement sent the cab crashing against another carriage.

In a moment, all was confusion and shouting. The driver, cursing, leaped from his seat and went to calm his horse, which was plunging dangerously. A crowd of happy people, eager to help, hinder, and tell just exactly what had happened, gathered within moments. Harry, rather shaken, was kindly but roughly pulled from the wrecked cab by half a dozen willing hands.

'You all right, guv?' The driver turned from his horse to check his fare. 'Dashed if I've ever done that before. Took me mind off me driving, didn't you, with your hurry, hurry, drive faster. Now you see where all that rushing gets us! You'll have to pay me the price of me cab, guv, and that's a fact.'

Harry was horrified. 'I can't,' he stammered, brushing off the helping hands. 'And anyway, it's your job to watch out for other traffic on the roads.'

'That's the nobs for you,' remarked the driver bitterly to the world at large. 'Here I am, an honest working man, trying to get an honest crust for my wife, as good a woman as ever breathed, and a bunch of kids. Now I've lost me cab, and who's to look after 'em now?'

'You've still got the horse,' said Harry weakly, trying to stem the flood of eloquence that was raising murmurs of sympathy from the assembled bystanders.

'And what use is a horse to me, may I ask?' replied the man with awful sarcasm. 'Nothing but worry and expense, a horse is, if it can't be earning its keep. A horse without a cab to pull, I mean ter say, wot good's that?'

The crowd certainly seemed to be turning against Harry, who was at a loss what to do.

'Look here, I'm sorry, and all that, and I'd help if I could, I really would.'

'Help-if-I-could won't feed me starving children,' returned the cabbie, who was beginning to enjoy himself. His children were all, in fact, in full employment, and well able to fend for themselves. The cab, too, now that he came to look at it properly, would not be too difficult to repair. Still, he had the crowd on his side, and there was no harm in milking this young toff all he could. He drew breath to continue, but a new voice interrupted him.

'I think you may be over-stating your case a little, cabbie,' came the calm, measured tones.

Harry looked up in relief, and recognised his saviour with astonishment. 'Atherington! It is you, isn't it?'

'It is indeed, St Erth. Are you hurt?'

'Not in the least, I thank you, though my clothes are rather the worse for wear.' He ruefully surveyed the dust and rents that the accident had inflicted on his best coat. 'The thing is, this man seems to think I should pay for his cab!'

'Oh, why, were you driving?' Sir Robert's calculated look of astonishment brought a laugh from the turncoat crowd, more interested in entertainment than anything else, and with an instinct for justice also.

'No, but I spoke to him, and he says he was distracted.'

'Dear me! You should write a placard, fellow, to say that you will only carry fares who are deaf and dumb.' This brought another laugh, and the cabbie took refuge in bluster.

'He kept telling me to hurry, sir, and he seemed that worried, I was trying to get there as fast as I could. I thought he must be going to some sick person, or some such, and I likes to do me best for my fellow man . . .'

'That will do.' Robert, accustomed to command, allowed a hint of steel to enter his voice, and the driver gave up. Robert turned to the crowd. 'You have had your fun, now it is over, and you should be about your business. You, fellow, take this,' there was a chink of coins and the driver touched his hat, 'and be thankful that this gentleman does not make formal complaint of your careless driving. Come, St Erth.'

'Thank you, sir . . . you are very kind. You must allow me to repay . . . when I am able, that is . . .'

'Not at all, the merest trifle. Now we shall clean you up, and you shall tell me where you were going in such a rush. Surely you should be in Oxford still?'

Harry groaned, the memory of his mission returning with horrid suddenness. 'I must get to Grosvenor Square!' he cried.

'But not looking like that! You would frighten them all into fits. Come, St Erth. I think you had better tell me what this is all about.' Not unwilling to pour his problems into an older ear, Harry accompanied Robert to his nearby lodgings.

CHAPTER EIGHTEEN

BARTON WAS worried about his master. He had been
pleased, when Robert returned from his stay at the farm,
to see how much better he was looking. He had also been
pleased to discover that the nightmares, that unwelcome
legacy from the Crimea, were almost a thing of the past.
The journey to London was, he assumed, no more than a
formality, to confirm something that had already happened. No more than Robert did he expect his master's suit
to be unwelcome to the Earl and his family, and he assumed that her father's permission was all that would be
required. An engagement, to be followed fairly soon by a
bridal, was what he had in mind, and then the Captain
would settle down at Atherington for good.

Now, however, settling down seemed to be the last thing
on the Captain's mind. After the restlessness of the first
few days when he could not get to see Harriet, he had gone
to her ball in an almost visible aura of happiness, only to
return later the following day with a face like thunder.
Since then he had scarcely spoken to his manservant, who
merely guessed that something had gone amiss. He found
that he was hurt that his master did not confide in him,
though he knew this to be unreasonable. They had been
more like friends than master and man, since the war, but
there are some things that a man finds it hard to speak of,
even to his friends, and of these things his dealings with a
lady were most likely to be kept secret. Barton could only

wonder what had happened. A refusal by the Earl, while it might annoy, would not have provoked such a strong reaction, and anyway Barton could see no reason for the Earl to refuse. Barton rightly guessed that Robert's anger, and the resulting return of his nightmares, meant that the lady herself had rejected him.

Barton was determined to find out more, and if necessary to do something about it. Not for this had he fought, in Scutari, for his master's life. He would not allow some society Miss, as he thought of her, to destroy the life that he, Barton, had saved. Determined to help but not knowing how to go about it, in his desperation he took to following the Captain when he went out. It was not difficult. His master's above average height made him stand out in the crowds, as did his military bearing. Also, Robert was so lost in his own thoughts that the man sometimes thought he would not have noticed if he had followed him a mere pace behind his heels.

It did not take him long to discover that Robert visited the house in Grosvenor Square daily, but that he did not stay long enough for a proper visit to have taken place. Careful reconnoitering revealed a houseful of ladies, one of them very pretty. Barton, seeing the lovely Amanda coming out of the house with her mother and sister, could be forgiven for assuming that she, and not Harriet, was his master's chosen lady.

The following day he loitered in the square until he saw Robert leave the house. Allowing a quarter of an hour to elapse, he went to the servants' entrance in the area and knocked. It had not escaped his notice that Robert and the butler had met and parted with more warmth than was usual in such an establishment. He was in luck. Giving the story he had prepared about his master's missing pair of gloves, Barton was told that the butler was at that moment in the staff sitting room next to the kitchen. Barton was ushered in. He offered again the story of the mislaid gloves.

'I do not think, Mr Barton, that the gloves were left Here,' said the butler at his most butlerish. 'I am always very careful about Callers' Belongings. Besides, Sir Robert came no further than the hall, as I was obliged to inform him that Lady Harriet was Not At Home.'

'I am afraid,' said Barton, 'that the Captain—Sir Robert, I should say—is sadly absent-minded of late. I am sure I meant no reflection on the care you take, for my master has often remarked to me on the excellent way you carry out your duties, Mr . . . er . . . ?'

'Crowborough is the name, Mr Barton,' the butler supplied, unbending at the compliment. 'It is a very warm day. Won't you take a seat, Mr Barton, and join me in a little glass of something?' Nothing loath, Barton sat down, and accepted a glass of sherry. They sipped in silence, Barton waiting respectfully for the other man to take up the conversation.

'Absent-minded, is he?' mused Crowborough, offering a plate of biscuits to his guest. 'Will you take a biscuit with your sherry?'

'Thank you, Mr Crowborough, I will. If I may say so, a most excellent glass of sherry. Yes, very absent-minded.'

'Thank you, Mr Barton. We pride ourselves on the quality of Our wines, although the cellar is not as well stocked as We would like to see it. A gentleman in love, Mr Barton, is inclined to be absent-minded. Particularly if the course of love does not, as the saying goes, run smooth.'

'I can see, Mr Crowborough, that I need hide nothing from you. My master is not a happy man. Not only is he forgetful, he is irritable. And I can tell you, that in all the years I have known the Captain, I have never known him to be irritable.'

'You have been with him for some time, then, Mr Barton? In the army, I suppose.'

'I was his batman during the war, and before that I was in service with his family. I thought I knew the Captain—Sir Robert, I mean—inside out. But he's a changed man, Mr Crowborough, a changed man!'

'I won't hide from you, Mr Barton, that I have made it my business to become acquainted with your master. He calls here most days, as you may know. I saw what was in the wind that first evening, the night of the ball, when I saw how he and Lady Harriet looked at one another. We are all fond of Lady Harriet in this household. A very pleasant-spoken young lady, we have always found her. I think I may tell you that she is not happy, either.'

Barton leaned forward. 'Have you any idea what may have gone wrong, Mr Crowborough? My master came to London as happy as a king, and I saw then that there was love in the air. It seems they met in the country, and all was well until the day after the ball.'

'All I can tell you, Mr Barton, is that he saw the Earl, my master, and then Lady Harriet alone. They were in the library for no more than ten minutes, and then my lady was running up the stairs, and his lordship was shouting, and there has been no peace in this house ever since. A lover's quarrel, I said to myself. I told your master, don't give up, sir, I said. Lady Harriet, she's very set in her ways when she makes up her mind, but don't you give up. He took my advice, and calls here, but will she see him?' Wisely interpreting this as a rhetorical question, Barton contented himself with shaking his head. 'No, she will not. I tell you, Mr Barton, something must be done, for I can see for myself she's fretting away to nothing.'

He gave Barton a second glass of sherry, and they sipped in thoughtful silence. Barton finished his glass, and put it down carefully. He looked at the butler. 'If she won't see the Captain,' he said slowly, 'will she see me?'

'See you?' Crowborough was surprised, but did not appear to be shocked.

Encouraged, Barton continued. 'It seems to me that she's got some wrong idea about my master. When he was staying at your Home Farm, he wanted to be incognito, if you understand me, so he didn't tell them his real name. Mr Roberts, he was known as.'

'No harm in that, Mr Barton, that I know of.'

'So I would have thought, but young ladies are different. If I could see her, and explain things to her . . . no one knows him better than I.'

The butler was silent for several minutes. 'It's irregular, Mr Barton. It could cost me my job. But I think it might work. You're a man after my own heart. I'll be damned if I don't do it!'

'We could have done with a few more of your sort in the Crimea,' said Barton gratefully. 'A man of vision, a man of action, Mr Crowborough! When shall it be?'

'That's the difficulty, Mr Barton. The ladies are out a good deal, of course, and it's seldom you can catch Lady Harriet on her own. As it happens, her ladyship has gone out this morning, and this very moment would have been a good time, only I know for a fact that Lady Harriet is to spend the morning with Lady Beatrice.'

'Lady Beatrice! That wouldn't be Lady Beatrice Fitzpaine, would it?'

'The very same. You know her?'

'Know her? I should think I do! She is my master's aunt, or great-aunt. She was the first person he visited when we came back to England, and when she came to London the other day she came to see us, and I poured her a glass of madeira with my own hands. And now she's staying here!'

Crowborough looked at him.

'It seems to me there's more to this than I thought. Lady Beatrice has never stayed with us before, that I can remember. Surely she is here for the same purpose that you are, to persuade my young lady to change her mind.'

'Then I need not do any more.'

'I don't know about that, Mr Barton. Lady Beatrice has been keeping to her room since she arrived, for she went down with a nasty cold, and at her age, I need hardly tell you, she has to take every precaution. I am positive that Lady Harriet has not spoken to her at all. Nor am I sure that her ladyship will succeed.' He cogitated, twisting his empty glass round and round in his fingers. Then he surged to his feet. 'If you do not take it amiss, Mr Barton, I think that we could not do better than to speak to Lady Beatrice herself. I have found her to be a very pleasant lady, strict, but straightforward to deal with. Since we are all fighting, as it were, on the same side, it seems to me that a council of war is called for.'

He left the room, and returned some minutes later.

'Her ladyship is of the opinion, Mr Barton, that Lady Harriet is more likely to take notice of what you say, than of her. She bids me tell you that she has complete confidence in you, and that she will see Lady Harriet afterwards, and do what she can to further things. With your permission, I will call Lady Harriet at once, before she goes to her ladyship's room.'

Crowborough made his stately way up to the small sitting room where Harriet and Amanda were chatting in a desultory way. He cleared his throat.

'Yes, Crowborough, what is it?' asked Harriet. 'Is someone here? I did not hear the door.'

'Someone is here, my lady, who would like to speak to you, if you would be so kind. You did not hear the door, because he came to the servants' entrance. He is by way of being a gentleman's gentleman, rather than a gentleman, my lady.' This tortuous sentence caused Harriet to knit her brows, and Amanda to giggle.

'Good gracious, whoever can it be? Does he want to see me, myself, or will anyone do?'

'I fancy it is you yourself, my lady. He has something of a very private nature to discuss with you.'

'Can you tell me what it is about, Crowborough?'

'I fear not, my lady. But I think I can say that you need not hesitate to admit him. I can vouch for him myself. His motive in coming is most selfless.'

'Well, it all sounds very mysterious. I do not see how you can possibly refuse,' said Amanda cheerfully, gathering up her belongings. 'As his business is private, I had better leave you, but I shall be near by if you call.' She left the room gracefully, and Crowborough went to fetch Barton. Harriet waited for his return in some trepidation.

'Mr Barton, my lady,' announced the butler, his habitual ringing tones rather subdued.

'Thank you, Crowborough. Good morning, Mr Barton. I understand you wanted to speak to me. Will you sit down?' She indicated a chair, but Barton remained on his feet.

'Thank you, my lady, but I'd as soon stay standing, if you don't mind. I don't think I could feel comfortable, sitting down in here with you.' He looked round the little room, full of knickknacks and trifles of embroidery, decorated with posies of flowers sent by Harriet's admirers. His gaze returned to Harriet, who was watching him in some amusement as he gravely examined her.

'Begging your pardon, my lady, but you are the Lady Harriet Milborne?'

Harriet laughed. 'So I have always believed.'

Barton looked sheepish. 'It's just that I saw you once leaving the house with her ladyship, and another young lady, and I thought...' He did not know how to continue. Harriet helped him out.

'You saw my sister Amanda and thought she was I? She is much prettier than I, is she not?'

'That's not for me to say, my lady, but there's the saying, handsome is as handsome does.' He gave her another searching look, which Harriet returned with placid candour. 'It seems to me, my lady, that you would not be the kind of young woman who wouldn't want to listen to what a man has to say, just because that man's a servant.'

Harriet looked grave. 'I hope I should listen to anyone, whoever they were, if what they had to say was true, and honest.'

'As the day, my lady! Do you believe me?'

'I believe I do. You look like the sort of man who can be trusted. Trust me too, then, and tell me what it is you want.'

'I am afraid you will not be pleased, my lady. I am manservant to Sir Robert Atherington.' She made as if to rise, but he stopped her with a gesture. 'Let me speak, I beg you, my lady. The Captain, I mean, Sir Robert, he doesn't know I'm here. I think he would half kill me if he knew. But I've been with him many years, my lady. I was with him in the Crimea. He saved my life, and I saved his when he was wounded, and in the hospital. I know him through and through, my lady, and a better man never lived. And I can't bear to see him getting thin again, and crying out in the night with the dreams I thought he'd put behind him.'

His voice was hoarse with emotion. Harriet had turned away her head, so that her face was hidden behind her hair, which was but loosely tied into a soft knot at the nape of her neck. She did not speak, but he saw her tremble, and with renewed courage he continued to speak.

What he said, with simple words and heartfelt honesty, opened her mind and heart to admit that the Robert she knew, Mr Roberts, was the true Robert, whatever he called himself. He told her, not just of the Crimea, as Robert had done, but of how he had been there. Small acts of kindness and compassion, greater acts of heroism, all of which he had glossed over or suppressed, were laid before her. His sufferings, not just for himself, but for his men, revealed, and his deep and urgent need for peace and solitude made clear as never before. She saw that she had misjudged him, had failed him at the time when he most needed her, and she wondered if she could ever forgive herself, or if he could ever forgive her.

When Barton at length finished speaking, she could not answer. She could scarcely move. Her hands tightly clenched, her back rigid, she was ashamed to look at him in the face. He, not knowing whether she were moved or merely angry, crept quietly from the room. He had done all he could. Outside on the landing Crowborough looked a question, and Barton shook his head in ignorance. In silence the two conspirators crept downstairs, and out through the kitchen door. Barton, still speechless, shook the butler by the hand, and turned away. Crowborough returned to stand, listening, at the foot of the stairs. The house was silent, not a voice, not a movement. Sighing, he returned to his quarters in the basement.

CHAPTER NINETEEN

RETURNING TO the lodgings, Barton had been relieved to find that his master had not been aware of his absence. Robert had, in fact, taken advantage of a fine morning to stroll in the Park on his way home. He had become used to regular physical exercise while working on the farm, and found his London existence far too static. Barton hoped very much that he had not done more harm than good, and was particularly attentive to his master's wishes, ordering dishes for his dinner that he knew were favourites, and keeping as low a profile as was possible. He wondered very much what Lady Beatrice would say to the young lady, and whether she, too, would not do harm.

He need not have worried. Summoned to her ladyship's bedchamber soon after Barton left, Harriet went with none of the anxiety she would otherwise have felt at meeting Robert's great-aunt for the first time. So taken up was her mind with what she had heard, that she was hardly aware of her surroundings. She found Lady Beatrice sitting up in bed, very smart in a Kashmir shawl and a night-cap of awe-inspiring beauty. Giving a schoolgirl curtsy and uttering the wish that Lady Beatrice was quite recovered, Harriet found her reception not at all what she had been fearing.

'There you are, my dear child,' said Lady Beatrice, stretching out a beringed hand. 'Come over here and give me a kiss. Goodness, what eyebrows! Your mama told me they were dark, but I had no idea! No, do not be affronted, my dear. They lend a great deal of character to your face. And with a nose like mine, how could I criticise you!'

Disarmed by this open approach, Harriet planted an obedient kiss on the proffered cheek, and obeyed a gesture to seat herself on the edge of the bed.

'You need have no fear of taking my cold, for I find myself much recovered today. Indeed, I pride myself that I am in the pink of health for my age.'

'Yes, ma'am, I can see that,' said Harriet with a responsive twinkle. 'I think when you are downstairs again you will put us all to shame. Mama tells me you will accompany us to the Embersleys' dance next week. Shall you dance, Lady Beatrice?'

'No, my dear, I leave all that sort of thing to you, and I am sure you do it very prettily. What is this I hear about you, that you are started on a brilliant season of conquests? Lord Istead has been very particular in his attentions, and of course there is my poor nephew Robert.'

Harriet flushed, and muttered something indistinguishable.

'Never fear, dear child, I am not come to scold you! No, I am sure you are doing the right thing. Nothing could be more distasteful than to marry where there is not love, and besides, I am sure you can do better for yourself. Robert is all very well, but Lord Istead would be considered by many a far better catch. So very rich, and of course the title. You would have your own way, too, I should think, for he would be no match for those eyebrows, and a complaisant husband, child, is not to be sneezed at.'

Her bright eyes looked sharply at Harriet, who hardly knew how to answer her. This was not at all the sort of thing she had expected to hear from her mother's godmother, particularly since she was also Robert's great-aunt.

'I should not wish to make Sir Robert unhappy,' she ventured.

'Unhappy? He'll soon get over that, my dear. There are plenty of young ladies who will be only too happy to console him. I shouldn't give him another thought, if I were you.' Lady Beatrice then determinedly turned the subject to affairs of the day, and kept Harriet talking for the rest of the morning. She was pleased to find Harriet's good manners would not allow her to return to a subject which Lady Beatrice could see only too well was occupying her mind almost to the exclusion of anything else, and she also delighted in Harriet's knowledge of political matters, and in her sudden flashes of wit that even her misery did not suppress.

Harriet left the visitor's bedchamber feeling completely wrung out. Robert console himself with another girl? Not if she could help it. And as for Lord Istead . . . she almost ground her teeth and she remembered Lady Beatrice counselling her to accept him. She would sooner die! When the door was shut Lady Beatrice herself sank back on her pillows, almost as tired as Harriet. She smiled a satisfied smile. It was a long time since her own salad days, but she had not forgotten how a young girl's mind worked.

Barton saw Robert leave the following morning with a mixture of hope and anxiety. He was fairly sure that Robert was once again going to call at the house in Grosvenor Square, and wondered whether this time Lady Harriet would agree to see him.

He was therefore all the more surprised when Robert returned, after only a short time, with a strange young gentleman who looked as if he might have been in a fight.

'My friend Viscount St Erth has had the misfortune to be involved in an accident in a cab,' Robert explained. 'Will you see what you can do?'

'Certainly, sir. This way, if you please, my lord.'

'But there's no time...' protested Harry.

Barton was firm. Viscount he might be, but hardly more than a boy, and him with dust on his clothes and a bloody scratch on his face! 'Just a few moments, my lord, to wash your face, and give me a chance to brush the dirt off your clothes. You'll be surprised how much better you'll feel.'

'And I think perhaps a drop of brandy, don't you, Barton?'

'Just what I was about to suggest, Captain.' Harry, feeling every minute more like a naughty schoolboy, was taken firmly away to be tidied up. When he returned he was much cleaner, and the brandy had done away with the extreme pallor Robert had noticed.

'Feeling better?'

'Oh yes, thank you. Your man is a good chap, isn't he? Got me tidied up in no time.'

'He has had plenty of practice at that. He always managed to keep my uniform cleaner than anyone else's, God knows how.'

'You were in the Crimea together, were you not? I noticed he called you Captain, and he said to me it should have been Major. I—I should like of all things to hear about that, some time. Only not now!' His diffident manner vanished as he once again recalled the object of his journey.

'I wish you would sit down, and tell me what is worrying you,' said Robert mildly. 'I might be able to help you, you know.'

'It's very good of you, sir, but I don't know why you should bother with me. You don't even know me. Besides, you can't help me. I don't think anyone can!'

Robert had to suppress a smile at his tone of extreme despair. 'I shouldn't be too sure of that. As for why I should help you, have you forgotten that I aspire to the status of brother-in-law to you? Who knows but what Harriet might change her mind, if she knows I have helped you.' He spoke in jest, seeing that Harry was hesitating, reluctant to admit to a comparative stranger, however friendly, how foolishly he had behaved. 'I think it only right to tell you,' he said gently, 'that your sister did in some sort confide in me, before we had our—difference of opinion.' He saw that Harry was bristling angrily, and continued in haste. 'It was wrong of her, I know, and I tried to stop her. But you must understand that we had always been completely open with one another, except in one respect which I can only bitterly regret. Your sister looked on me as a member of the family. I should also say that I did not agree with the feelings she expressed on the subject.'

Harry drew a deep breath. 'Well, I can't deny that I don't like to think of her telling you, but I suppose someone has got to know sooner or later, and I'd rather it were you than Papa, or Mama.'

He launched into the full tale, omitting no detail. Robert heard him out in peace, for he could see what a relief it was to the boy to be able to tell it all. Harriet was all very well, but to be able to discuss it with a man—and one who, he was sure, would neither ridicule nor blame him, was wonderful.

Robert nodded, listened, and felt about a hundred and ten. Had he ever been like this boy? He supposed he had, once, long ago, before he went into the army. A romantic passion for someone totally unsuitable was, he was well aware, a normal part of many boys' development. Harry was no different from thousands of his kind, and better than most, for he was only too happy to compensate Annie for any disappointment she might have suffered, so far as he could. Robert felt that in the fullness of time Harry would make a good earl. Now it was up to him to see that the episode did not sour the boy's essential sweetness of character, but instead served to make him more sympathetic towards the weakness of others.

He spoke, and Harry listened. Not rebelliously as he might have done if Robert had been angry with him, or made him feel a fool.

'You have no responsibility towards this girl, St Erth. If, as you say, your relationship was an innocent one, she has nothing at all to complain of. The poems? If a man had to marry every girl he wrote a poem to, we should all have to turn followers of the Prophet, and keep harems. If you had said you wanted to be her slave, would that give her the right to sell you?'

'I suppose not. But her father said he would take me to court, and the publicity... Mama and Papa would never get over it.'

'Take you to court? I should like to see him try! Depend upon it, he has no such intention, for he knows he would be laughed out of court. My dear boy, you are under age. Didn't you know that no action for Breach of Promise may be brought against a minor?'

Harry turned first white, then pink with shock and relief. 'You mean, I need not have worried?'

'You need certainly not have worried about having to stand trial. The man sounds a nasty piece of work, however, and the threat to go to your father is a real one. Even without a Breach of Promise action, the newspapers would be happy to report such a scandal, if there were any written proof.'

'I know my father would understand, and stand up for me.'

'Of course he would. I do not know him very well, but he struck me as being both kind and generous, particularly where his children are concerned.'

'He is the best of parents,' said Harry warmly.

'The trouble is that in his generosity, and his anxiety to protect you, he might be tempted to make a payment to this man, to save you from him. That would never do.'

'No, indeed! Poor Papa, when he has so many expenses already with the girls.'

'Not only that. It would be a great mistake to let this— Chorlton, you say?—benefit from his schemes. One payment would certainly not be enough for him, and who knows where it would end? Besides, if the girl is as lovely as you say, and I can quite believe she is, what is to stop him from moving to some other city, and doing the same thing all over again to some other fellow? So they might live for some years, until she no longer kept her first beauty. Then, I am afraid, her end would not be a good one. Would you put it past him, when she was of less use to him, to sell her to the highest bidder? And after a wandering life such as they must lead, with her delicacy of feeling hardened by the deceptions she would be forced to use, can you be sure she would not let him, and so sink at last into a life of shame?'

Harry was much impressed. 'Poor little Annie! You are quite right, for though she is truly innocent now, how could such a life as you describe fail to blunt her sensibilities? She has not known a mother's care for many years, for Mrs Chorlton died when she was quite a child, and has had no one to guide her but that scoundrel.'

'Then it is amazing that she is still as innocent as you say, and speaks well for her innate good sense and feeling. The temptations for a beautiful girl in such a city as Oxford, must be considerable, even with a mother's watchful eye on her. You would, then, be willing that she be helped, if in so doing we could keep her away from her father, or at least see that the money is not used by him?'

'Certainly. I always meant to do my best for her.'

'Then I think you may safely leave it in my hands. No,' he held up his hand as Harry started to protest, 'you must allow me to help you now, as your future brother-in-law. If Harriet still refuses to marry me, you may repay me at your leisure, when you can do so. Say no more! My mind is quite made up. I shall come to Oxford, and see them myself. You need have no fear of their bothering your parents!

Harry leaped to his feet. 'But they are not in Oxford! My God, I was busy telling you how we met that I forgot to give you the reason for my journey. They are here, in London, and perhaps even now at Grosvenor Square!'

'When did they leave?'

'I don't know,' cried Harry, feverishly searching his pockets and dragging out Annie's crumpled letter. 'I didn't read this until this morning, but it was delivered some time last night. I went out on the river with some friends, and was late back, so I didn't see it until I awoke.'

He held out the letter to Robert, who ran his eyes over it swiftly. Harry would have run straight out into the street and off to Grosvenor Square on foot, if Robert had not held him back.

'Wait! Let me think. No good purpose can be served by your going there. If they have not yet arrived, which I suppose we may still hope for, though it seems unlikely, you are not needed. If they are, your presence can only add to your parents' discomfort, and make your father more likely to pay up.'

'What can I do! I cannot stay skulking here!'

'You must go straight back to Oxford.' Harry looked mutinous and Robert could have shaken him, but forced himself to reason instead. 'Listen, St Erth. Did you have leave to come to London this morning?'

'Of course not! What possible reason could I have given? I only just escaped being gated last time, when I stayed too long after Hetty's ball. Besides, there was no time. I just dressed and ran for the train.'

'Then think what it will mean if it is discovered that you have come up to London once again, scarcely more than a week since that last time! How pleased would your father be, do you suppose, if you are sent down for the rest of the term? Besides, if the authorities find out that you had a letter from a lady—and don't tell me that your scout wouldn't have seen that at once from the handwriting— and then went haring up to London, what sort of a scandal-broth might not ensue?'

Harry had to agree that there was something in what he said.

'Then be a good fellow and take the first train back to Oxford. Tell your scout that it was all a mistake, make him believe it, get back to your books, and pray to all that's holy that no one saw you on the train. Will you do that?'

Reluctantly Harry agreed that he would. He hated to feel that he was running away from trouble but he had to admit that the trouble was likely to be twice as bad for everyone if he showed his face in Grosvenor Square.

Robert saw him off, snatching a newspaper as he did so and thrusting it into Harry's hand. 'Here, keep your head down until you get to the train, then try to find an empty carriage and keep your face behind this. It would never do to be spotted now!'

Harry gave a reluctant grin, shook his benefactor warmly by the hand and departed, promising an instant amendment of life and the future behaviour of a saint.

Robert hoped the resolve would not last too long. He had no fancy to be brother-in-law to a prig. As Harry disappeared down the road, Robert took up his own hat and gloves.

'You are going out, sir?' asked Barton, who was consumed with curiosity to know what was happening.

'Yes,' said Robert. 'I am going to Grosvenor Square. I may be some time—in fact, I do not know when I will be back. I have to deal with a dragon. Not a very large dragon, but one with a bit of fire to breathe, all the same.'

Barton struggled with a broad grin. 'Very good, Captain, sir. And may I say, as one old soldier to another, good hunting, and the best of luck!'

'Thank you, Barton. I think I may very well need it.' Placing his hat at a jaunty angle on his head, Robert strode from the house. He felt inordinately cheerful. For good or ill, the time was come to make the final assault. His tactics might perhaps be considered a little devious, he supposed, but had not Harriet herself implored him to help her brother? He wondered what his darling girl had written to Annie, his lips curling into a smile as he pictured her dismay when they landed up on her doorstep. However much she might dream of a romantic love-match between her brother and his lovely shopgirl, the reality might, he thought, make her think again. Reaching Grosvenor Square he took the steps two at a time, and beat a resounding tattoo on the front door.

CHAPTER TWENTY

HARRIET HAD passed an uncomfortable night. Every word that Barton had spoken had seemed to echo round her brain, and when she did at length fall into a troubled sleep, her dreams were full of them. That she should have behaved so unkindly, so unfairly! She blushed to remembered her behaviour. She had been in love with a dream, and part of that dream had been her own secret pride that she, the daughter of an Earl, should condescend to marry a man so far beneath her own station in life. She saw now that her fury at being deceived had stemmed, in large part, from having to relinquish that dream. An ordinary, unremarkable marriage with a man of whom her family and society would approve, was not exciting enough for her. She had almost wanted to shock, to rebel and she had hidden it even from herself under a veil of acting without prejudice. And in so doing she had been more prejudiced than anyone else. Now, worse than all, here was Lady Beatrice suggesting that she marry Lord Istead! To her fevered imagination it seemed likely that the Earl and Countess would do the same, and that in her weakened state she might even agree to it.

She did not know how she could face Robert. She knew, of course, that he had continued to call almost every day. Often she had had to fight a longing to watch, from behind the curtains of an upstairs window, and see his tall, well-loved figure entering and leaving the house. She had only to tell the butler and she could see him, perhaps that very morning. He would be angry, of course, and he would have every right to be. Would he then forgive her? She could not be sure of it. Would she have been able to, if the positions were reversed? She was afraid not. And yet she had to try.

She arose in the morning pale and heavy eyed. Lady Cornelia took one look at her, and sent her back to her room.

'I shall certainly not take you out looking like that,' she said firmly. 'You look the colour of skimmed milk, and there are great dark marks beneath your eyes. Have you the headache again?'

'Not really, Mama,' responded Harriet listlessly. 'I am afraid I did not sleep very well last night.'

'Then you had better go back to bed, and try to sleep now,' said the Countess with practical kindness. 'I do not usually advocate such habits, as you know, but do not forget we are to go to the Opera tonight, with the Duchess and her party. You must be in better looks by then, for it would never do to show such a wan face to the world.'

'I am sorry, Mama,' said Harriet, thinking that she seemed to spend most of her time apologising to her parents.

'Well, I do not wish to reproach you with what is now past, but if you are not happy it seems to me that you have no one but yourself to blame. However, on that subject I shall be dumb. Now do not cry, Harriet, or you will look worse than ever.'

Harriet went miserably back to her room but did not, however, go back to bed as her mother had recommended. The memory of her dreams hung over her mind like a miasma, and she dreaded their return if she once laid her head back on the pillow. Instead she fidgeted about, picking up random objects and putting them down again elsewhere, to the intense if unexpressed annoyance of her maid, who was putting away her clothes and sorting those that needed washing or mending.

Harriet waited until the bustle that signified her mother's departure from the house had ceased, then went down to the hall to look for Crowborough. He was scandalised.

'You shouldn't be coming down here after me, my lady. It's not fitting. If you had rung, I should have come up to you.'

'I wanted to be sure of speaking to you privately, Crowborough. Sir Robert Atherington calls here most mornings, doesn't he?'

'Yes, my lady. Do you wish me to tell him you are not at home, as usual?'

'No. I—I shall see him today, Crowborough. I shall be in the small sitting-room. Please bring him up.'

'Very good, my lady.' Crowborough could not keep the satisfaction out of his voice.

Harriet looked at him shyly, knowing that like all good servants he would know as much, if not more, of what was afoot than members of the family. 'I have been very silly, haven't I, Crowie?'

The use of her childhood's nickname for him softened him completely. 'Not really, my lady. Just rather young, and that's to be expected at your time of life, isn't it? Don't you fret, I'll bring him up straight away. And if I may make so bold, I think he'll be a happy man when I tell him.'

Harriet blushed, and went back up the stairs. Crowborough watched her fondly as she retreated. A good girl, he thought. Not beautiful, maybe, but a good girl all the same.

Harriet waited in the little sitting room. The house was very quiet. The Earl had gone to his club to meet some like-minded cronies, the Countess was out with Amanda, the children were at their lessons. Lady Beatrice still kept to her room, though it was rumoured that she would be down very shortly. Harriet took up a book and tried to read. The words danced in front of her tired eyes, and she started at every footstep on the pavement outside. There was the sound of wheels, and a little bustle. She sat frozen in her chair, like a terrified rabbit. The knock at the front door was almost drowned by the drumming of her heart. A man's voice, Crowborough's familiar tones in answer. She strained her ears. Surely it was he? Then the butler's measured tread up the stairs. She drew a deep breath, and gripped her hands together to keep them from trembling.

Crowborough came in, but his face was set in disapproving lines, and he did not have Robert with him. 'There is a Young Person to see you, my lady. She says you have invited her.' His tones were gloomily disgusted. After one look at Annie's finery and her father's suit, shiny at the seams, he would have denied them admittance, had they not shown him the beginning of a letter in Harriet's handwriting.

'A young person, Crowborough? To see me?' The surprise, coming after her expectation, was more than Harriet could take. She was completely at sea.

'A Young Female, my lady.'

'Is she alone?'

'No, my lady. She is accompanied by a . . . gentleman. Her father, I believe.' Crowborough was expert in conveying disapprobation without actually saying anything.

Much experience enabled Harriet to understand that the butler did not think that the young lady or her father were at all the sort of people who ought to be admitted to an Earl's establishment. The girl no better than she should be, in his opinion, and the father... well! If he didn't mean trouble, then he, Crowborough, was a monkey's uncle.

'Did they give no name?'

'They did, my lady. A Mr Chorlton, and Miss Chorlton. They had a letter, my lady.'

Harriet jumped to her feet in consternation. 'Chorlton! Good heavens, but that's...if anyone should meet them... Mama...
Where are they, Crowborough?'

'I left them in the hall, my lady, while I came to speak to you.' His tones spoke volumes. Trouble they were, and they would not set foot in any of the family's rooms, if he could help it. He had left them under the eye of the footman, just in case.

Harriet looked distracted. 'If Papa were to come home, or Mama... You must bring them up here, Crowborough. At once.'

'Up here, my lady?' The butler was scandalised. It was bad enough for Lady Harriet to have to speak to this young person in the hall, under his eye, but to bring her, and her doubtless disreputable father, up to the private sitting room! The house might be hired, but while the family resided there it had, in Crowborough's eyes, taken on the august gilding of nobility that permeated the Earl's own home.

Harriet almost stamped her foot in her anxiety. 'Oh, do not go all stuffy, Crowborough, pray! I cannot explain it to you, but it is very important that I see these people. I cannot risk my parents seeing them, so you must bring them up here. It will not be for long, I promise. Only do, please, be kind and bring them up here immediately!'

Crowborough could do no more than obey, though with many misgivings.

'Her ladyship will see you upstairs,' he announced frigidly to Annie and her father. 'Kindly follow me . . . Miss.' So dignified was his demeanour that Annie trembled as she climbed the stairs, and clutched at her father's arm. That worthy, however, was looking about him approvingly at the evidences of wealth displayed by the paintings on the walls, and the thick carpeting everywhere. He was in no way annoyed by Crowborough's behaviour; in fact, he would have been disappointed had he behaved in any other way. It entirely fitted his concept of the Earl's greatness that he, Chorlton, should be condescended to by the Earl's butler, and watched over by a six-foot footman as if he could not be trusted to keep his hands off the silver. In his way of thinking, the grander the Earl was, the more likely he was to pay a good sum to keep his son's name out of the gutter press. Unacquainted with high society, it did not occur to him that Crowborough had considerably higher standards than his employer, who at home was inclined to treat his tenants, his gamekeepers and other dependants as equals, if they showed a proper interest in his crops and his beasts.

'Miss Chorlton. Mr Chorlton,' announced the butler. 'I shall be very close by, my lady, if you should need me.' With a speaking look he withdrew.

Harriet stared at Annie. She thought that she had never seen so beautiful a girl, and she thought that no one could blame a young man for falling in love with her. Even Amanda, whom Harriet had been accustomed to thinking the loveliest girl she knew, paled against the guinea-gold hair, sapphire eyes and rose-petal complexion before her. Annie, for her part, was disappointed. She did not know quite what she had expected of an Earl's daughter, but this girl, though dressed with neatness and propriety, was not at all what she had envisaged. While she naturally was not so simple as to assume that the nobility went dressed in velvet and ermine every day, with coronets on their heads, nevertheless she had hoped for something rather special in the way of dresses. Harriet had dressed, after much thought, in an old gown of green dimity that Robert had once seen her in, and commented favourably on.

Since she had not been brought up, as Harriet had been, to hide her feelings, some of this was to be seen in her face. Harriet was in no way hurt. She had never thought of herself as even passably good-looking. With her usual good manners she came forward, holding out her hand.

'You must be Annie! And this is your Papa? How very…unexpected. But of course I am most pleased to see you. How very pretty you are, to be sure! Harry had told me so, and now I see he was right.' Annie blushed, and bobbed a curtsy. Mr Chorlton was looking Harriet over in a disagreeably assessing fashion, and she felt sure he was pricing her clothes and finding them disappointingly cheap. With the best will in the world to love the daughter, the father she could not like. She turned back to Annie.

'Will you not take off your jacket, and bonnet, as it is so warm today, and sit down? May I offer you refreshment?'

'Oh, no, I…' began Annie, but her father broke in.

'Your ladyship is most gracious. We should be glad of a little something, after our journey.'

'Of course. You have come up from Oxford today?' asked Harriet, ringing. Crowborough, looking even more dour, brought wine and cakes, and some early fruit from the glasshouses at home. Harriet tried to talk to Annie, but between awe at her surroundings, her promise to Pa to let him do the talking, and her fear of spilling something, or dropping crumbs on the carpet, that young lady was almost speechless.

Harriet turned to Mr Chorlton. 'Is there some way in which I can serve you?' she asked with gentle dignity.

'Your ladyship is very kind. My Annie was quite overwhelmed with gratitude when she got your letter. Such condescension in one so far above us! So when his Lordship said he would have no more to do with us, and my poor girlie was making herself ill from crying over him, I said, "my love, let us go and see her ladyship. She has professed herself your friend. Her feminine sensibilities will understand the pain her brother's thoughtlessness has caused. She will weep with you. She will comfort you. She will help you." And here we are,' he finished with unusual simplicity.

Harriet looked at Annie. She had blinked a little at the finery of her gown, and now thought that her perfect complexion had not been marred by very many tears.

'Are you so very unhappy?' she asked gently.

'Oh no,' said Annie thoughtlessly. She had in fact overcome her original shyness, and was now revelling in this experience of high life. To be sure Lady Harriet was nothing much, even if she was the daughter of an Earl, and as for her gown, Annie would not have worn it to do the marketing. Still, she had been served tea and cakes off a silver tray by a butler as grand as a Royal Duke, and her simple soul was satisfied.

'What my poor daughter means,' put in her father smoothly, with a look at Annie that boded no good for later, 'is that in her joy at your gracious reception, she has been able to forget her broken heart for a few moments. Why, only last night, she threatened to put a period to her existence, since his lordship had cast her aside.'

'Oh, Pa!' Annie was shocked. 'I never!'

'Be silent,' he ordered. 'Her ladyship must hear the truth.'

'I should certainly like to do that,' said Harriet, who by now had taken Mr Chorlton in strong aversion. 'I think that the best thing would be for Annie to tell it to me for herself.'

'Poor, foolish child,' he said with an attempt at fondness. 'She cannot bear to tell you how trusting she has been. And all through having such a loving heart, and so innocent a mind.'

Harriet was beginning to feel that here, too, she had been much mistaken. This girl, however pretty, could not be considered a suitable wife for Harry, with a father such as this. She began to regret her interference more and more, and could only hope that she could put things right.

'I sympathise with your disappointment, Annie, but are you sure that you really thought my brother would marry you? Did he actually propose to you?'

'Well, not really,' admitted Annie, unwilling in spite of her father's angry looks to give the lie outright. 'Only there were the poems, you see. And Pa said...'

'Pa said,' thundered that loving parent furiously, 'that he was not going to see his wronged child abandoned by her noble lover. Pa said, that if she is not given a handsome compensation, that those poems, and the letter in your own fair hand, my lady, would have to be given to the

Earl, or to whoever else can deal with such a scoundrel. And,' he added triumphantly, 'copies sent to every newspaper in the land. My daughter may not be slighted with impunity!'

'Oh, Pa, you promised!' shrieked Annie. 'You promised you wouldn't! Oh, oh, oh!' Her father gave her a great box on the ear, and she fell into strong hysterics.

Harriet sat frozen with horror. The door suddenly opened.

'What, may I enquire, is the cause of this dreadful noise? My good girl, if you shriek like that I shall be forced to throw some cold water over you. I don't know who you might be, sir, but I take leave to tell you that this is no way to conduct yourself in a gentleman's residence.'

Majestic in purple silk trimmed with jet, Lady Beatrice Fitzpaine stood at the open door and surveyed the scene before her. Harriet sank her face into her hands, and fought against an inclination to behave just as Annie had done.

It WAS at this moment that Robert's knock, so long awaited by Harriet but now unheard in the general pandemonium of the little upstairs sitting room, sounded on the front door. Crowborough hastened to open it, and his face of relief when he saw Robert was almost pitiful to behold. He nearly dragged Robert into the house and closed the door as if he was afraid that half the world would somehow follow him in and witness the shocking events that were taking place in his master's house.

'Sir Robert! Thank heaven it is you!' he gasped, his butler's calm for the first time in many years forsaking him.

'Yes, Crowborough, it is I,' said Robert soothingly. 'And not before time, it seems,' he added, cocking an ear to the sounds of discord that were only too distressingly plainly to be heard. 'Is Lady Harriet at home?' he inquired urbanely.

Crowborough cheered up for a moment. 'Yes, sir, and she came down specially to tell me that I was to bring you up to see her. I do believe she has had a change of heart, sir, and I hope to be the first to wish you very happy. She said I was to bring you straight up, sir, but now I don't know...'

'Did she indeed?' With maddening calm Robert continued to remove his gloves and lay them neatly with his hat on the table, since Crowborough was obviously too flustered to remember his usual duties. 'Was that before or after the arrival of the other guests?'

'Before, sir.' Crowborough did not know why he was wasting time talking. 'Will you come up now?' He clearly had great faith that his protégé could sort things out. 'The thing is, that I am not quite sure when Lady Cornelia or his Lordship might return...'

'Quite so. Yes, Crowborough my friend, I shall go up at once. You need not announce me.'

'Thank you, sir.'

With a cheerful air Robert ran up the stairs, while Crowborough withdrew to fortify himself with a stiff brandy. Robert had no need of directions, for though the door of the sitting room was closed such a noise was coming from behind it that he was in no doubt of which way to go. He raised his eyebrows in surprise as he heard the ringing tones of his great-aunt mingling with sobs from Annie, loud protests from her father, and soothing words from Harriet. His lips twitched—his beloved had by no means lost her head. She was attempting to calm Annie, and would probably have succeeded had it not been for the battle royal raging over their heads.

'Let me tell you, you horrid, vulgar little man, that you have no business in this house. No business in this house. No business at all.' Lady Beatrice, never one to mince her words, was making her feelings felt. Mr Chorlton, however, was her match for the moment, and was not to be daunted.

'No business! When I see my child, my only child, suffering before my eyes... I tell you, my fine lady, it is you who have no business here. Why, you ain't even one of the family.'

'That has nothing whatever to say to the matter. If the Earl or the Countess were here to see to things, I should of course have nothing to say to the matter.' Robert suppressed a laugh. He had never known his great-aunt not to have something to say in the affairs of any house in which she happened to be. 'Since they are absent, it behoves me, as their representative, to see that undesirable persons are not permitted to disrupt the house. As for your daughter's suffering, as you call it, she has no one to blame for it but herself, no doubt. And you. Any girl would suffer whose father cared only to make money out of her.'

Lady Beatrice was obviously well up to date with the situation. Robert was not surprised. He knew of old that his great-aunt's large nose had an infallible ability to sniff out scandals. He decided that it was time for him to intervene. He opened the door. Four faces were turned to him, and a momentary silence ensued.

'Good morning, Aunt Beatrice,' he said urbanely, advancing to kiss her cheek. 'Good morning, Lady Harriet. I trust I see you well?'

Harriet, whose face had lit in relief at the sight of him, paled again at this formal salute. He took pity on her.

'Do not bother to introduce me to your other guests, Lady Harriet. This I am sure is Mr Chorlton, and you are Annie, are you not, my dear? I had heard how lovely you are, and I see that I was not misinformed.'

Annie, her tears suspended by surprise, revived like a drooping flower in the sunshine of his flattery. She sat up, patted her hair, and surreptitiously pulled at the lace scarf to reveal rather more of her white shoulders than before. Harriet noticed with jealous irritation that even the storm of tears she had just undergone, and which had undoubtedly been genuine, did not dim her beauty. The reddened eyelids merely emphasised the deep blue of her eyes, and her cheeks were smooth and free of blotches. Harriet, who knew that her own face after her sleepless night and previous tears was pale, her eyes puffy and dark shadowed, could only feel that this was another instance of the unfairness of life.

'And who might you be?' blustered Mr Chorlton, seeing his control of the situation slipping.

'I don't think that need concern you, do you?' There was steel under the deceptive quietness of Robert's voice, and Chorlton took a step back. 'I was able to prevent—with some difficulty—the butler from sending for the police, as he was about to do when I arrived. I told him that I was sure you would not welcome being taken in charge, and that for your daughter's sake it must be hoped that it will not be necessary.'

'Police? There's no call for that sort of talk. You don't know anything about it, anyway. Police can't touch me.'

'I shouldn't be so sure of that, my good fellow. I know just about all there is to be known about this affair. And I should warn you that apart from making an affray in the Earl's residence, an offence for which they would be only too glad to take you away and charge you, there is also the more serious matter of trying to obtain money under false pretences. You are aware, I suppose, of the penalties of such an act?'

Mr Chorlton paled with anger. 'False pretences? I'll have you know, Mr Whoever you are, that it is no such thing. My daughter has been wronged, deeply wronged, and I have this letter to prove it.'

Advancing, he unwisely flourished Harriet's letter in Robert's face. With one swift movement Robert twitched it out of his hand, perused it rapidly, and tore it decisively into small pieces. In his rage Chorlton took a wild swing at his adversary, but found his own fist blocked by an arm that felt like a piece of oak, while another piece of oak, masquerading as a fist, caught him neatly on the chin in a punishing blow. He fell with a crash to the floor, and lay there stunned.

'Well, that was very neatly done, I must say, Robert,' said Lady Beatrice approvingly. 'I am not in general an advocate of violence, particularly in the presence of ladies, but in this instance I think I may say that you were completely justified.'

Annie looked at her father in horror. 'Oh, poor Pa! Is he dead?'

'I think that you will find that he is merely stunned,' Robert reassured her, feeling his adversary's head to check that he had not damaged his skull in the fall, and ascertaining that his breathing and heartbeat were steady.

'Oh, that's all right then.' She looked thoughtfully down at her father, and then up to Robert. 'I am sorry he tried to hit you, sir. He is not usually a violent man.'

'I am afraid I did provoke him, Annie. Now tell me, while you can speak without him interrupting, did you really expect to marry Viscount St Erth?'

'Oh, no,' she admitted candidly. 'When Pa said it, I did think I might like to, but I didn't really expect it.'

'He did not propose to you?'

'No, he was only a boy really. Very nice, of course, but not quite . . .'

'Quite so. Yet you allowed your father to threaten him?'

She hung her head. 'I am sorry, sir, and my lady. I knew I shouldn't. But he promised me he wouldn't really do it, and I did so want a bit of money.' She burst into tears, but more quietly this time.

Harriet went to her and put her arms round her. She spoke with sympathy. 'It was very wrong of you, but you are sorry now, aren't you? I know how easy it is to make mistakes, and to act in a way one afterwards regrets.' She did not look at Robert as she spoke, but he gave a little smile. 'Come, Annie, you will not cry any more, will you? I am sure Harry would not like it if you were unhappy, for though he might not want to marry you he does not want to hurt you.'

'On the contrary, he means well by you. I have seen him only this morning,' said Robert smoothly, ignoring Harriet's surprised look, 'and he was most grateful that you wrote to warn him of your father's intentions.'

'I'm glad I did, sir, and glad you tore up her ladyship's letter, too. I wouldn't want to cause any trouble, sir.'

'I can see that. By the way, where are the poems, Annie? Does your father have them with him?'

'Oh, they're all gone, sir,' said Annie blithely. 'I used them, sir, as curl papers. I didn't mean to, of course, but they were lying on the table, and I forgot they were important. Pa was that cross!'

Robert turned away to hide a smile, and a stifled giggle told him that Harriet was as amused as he.

'Then there is no more to be said. Your father appears to be coming back to his senses.' That individual was indeed beginning to stir and groan. 'Perhaps I had better give you this at once.' He handed Annie a small bundle of bank notes. Annie examined them in delight. 'For me? Oh, sir!' She hesitated. 'I don't feel I really deserve to have them, though. Not after all this trouble, and all.'

'Take the money, child,' put in Lady Beatrice unexpectedly. 'I can see that you have behaved a great deal better than I had thought at first, and if you did indeed warn St Erth that your father was coming, you have earned it, for I do not doubt that he will be very angry with you.'

'Yes, it is for you to keep,' agreed Robert. 'It is a gift from Viscount St Erth, in memory of your past friendship. But only for you, mind. There should be enough for you to leave your shop, should you wish to, and start a new life elsewhere. Do not, I implore you, let your father lay his hands on it.'

'Don't you worry, sir, I won't. I shall be able to set up a nice little millinery business, sir, like I've always wanted. And I'll keep Pa in order, never you fear. Ma always did so, when she was alive. I'll not let him use me again, sir. Will you thank his lordship for me? It's best if I don't see him again, and letter writing is something I was never too good at.'

'I shall tell him for you.'

Mr Chorlton opened his eyes, and felt his jaw tenderly. 'I could have you for assault,' he attempted thickly, but it was plain to be seen that all the bluster had gone out of him.

'I do not recommend you to try. Stand up, man, and let your daughter take you home. Be thankful that she is a good, dutiful girl, and will take care of you instead of having no more to do with you, as she might have done.'

Chorlton struggled to his feet, and Annie brushed off his clothes, which service he endured sullenly. She turned to Harriet, and curtsied. Harriet held out her hand.

'Thank you, my lady, for all your kindness. It was more than I deserved. I shall always remember you, and if I may make so bold, I wish you every happiness.'

'Thank you, Annie.' Harriet again avoided Robert's eyes. 'I am glad that all this has been resolved. I am sure you will make lovely bonnets—and maybe one day I shall come and buy one from you! You may always count on my friendship.'

'Spoken like a lady,' said Mr Chorlton with gloomy approval. 'Not like some I could mention.' He glared at Lady Beatrice, who had been watching the proceedings from an upright chair near the fireplace.

'Get along,' replied that redoubtable lady. 'You've caused enough trouble for one day.'

Still grumbling, Chorlton allowed his daughter to lead him from the room. Crowborough met them on the landing, where he had been hovering, and hustled them from the house, heaving a sigh of relief when he had once again closed the door. Thank heaven they were out of the way before his master or mistress returned. The mere thought of such a possibility made him feel quite weak at the knees, and he quickly took himself off in search of a further medicinal brandy. Then he thoughtfully swilled his mouth with peppermint, and returned to his post.

Meanwhile, in the upstairs sitting room, Lady Beatrice was once again congratulating Robert. 'You handled that very well, very well indeed. I don't pretend to understand the full ins and outs of the situation, but there is no doubt that that unpleasant man could have made a great deal of trouble—a great deal indeed. Young St Erth should be grateful to you.'

'I am sure he will be. At the moment I imagine he is in a state of some trepidation, wondering what has occurred. I must let him know as quickly as may be.'

'I suppose you supplied the money for that silly girl? I do not imagine that a young man of his age would be able to lay his hands on such a sum immediately.'

'Yes, but he is to repay me if—if necessary—when he is able to. It was not really so very much. And now, Aunt...'

But Lady Beatrice was not to be so easily put off. 'What do you mean, if necessary? Surely it is a debt of honour, and should be repaid as soon as possible?'

'No, just a loan to a friend. It is nothing to make a fuss about. Aunt, please...'

'In my young day, no gentleman...'

He interrupted her speech, his patience at an end. 'Aunt, I feel sure that after your cold it cannot be good for you to talk for so long.' He held open the door. 'Also I have something of a private nature—a very private nature—to say to Lady Harriet.'

She looked at the two of them, her beaky face softening into rare affection. 'Yes, I suppose you might have. Very well, I shall leave you.' She made her stately way to the door.

'You are all consideration, Aunt Beatrice,' he said.

She tapped his cheek with her mittened hand. 'That's right, be firm with her,' she said. 'It's time to put an end to all this shilly-shallying. If I were you...'

'Aunt, if you do not instantly leave this room...!'

'No need to take that tone with me, young man. I am not changing my mind all the time, and making a fuss about nothing. All right, I am going!' She was still talking as Robert closed the door behind her, and turned to face Harriet.

CHAPTER TWENTY-ONE

ROBERT LOOKED at Harriet in silence. She had turned away as Lady Beatrice was leaving the room, feeling that she did not know how to look at him. Now she turned back again, facing him bravely, and lifted her chin. Her hands were tightly clenched, and he saw with compunction the pallor of her face, and her shadowed eyes. It did not occur to him that she was looking plain. To him she was more beautiful in her sorrow than any woman could ever appear. He held out his hand to her.

'My poor girl,' he said. 'What a terrible morning this has been for you. I wish I could have arrived in time to have saved you this. Indeed, there are many sins of omission that are on my conscience, but I hope you will forgive them all.' His hand was still held to her, but she did not approach. In fact, she put her own hands behind her back as if to prevent them from coming to clasp his of their own accord. He stepped towards her, but she retreated and at once he stopped.

'No, Robert, let me speak. I must say it, though it is so hard. I have been stupid, and wicked, and foolish. I have treated you so badly, and in your generosity you came to my rescue, and Harry's. I can never forgive myself for what I have done.'

'Such harsh words,' he said tenderly, 'for so little a fault.'

'Little? How can you say so?'

He saw that she was overwrought, and had magnified her own error into gigantic proportions. He reasoned with her gently. 'A very little fault. You had much to provoke you. I know very well that I should have told you the truth from the first. If I had known, when we met, what you would come to mean to me, I would never have had such a secret from you. But even our friendship was unexpected. I had never thought that I could find such friendship with a woman. Love, yes, but not the comradeship that was ours.'

'I was living in a dream world,' she said bitterly.

'If you were, then so was I. I did not want to face up to life, to my responsibilities. But Harriet, what we had in that dream-world was so good, and true. Need it be only a dream? We are both awake now, as you might say, and I for one feel no differently about you than before. Our dreams are part of ourselves.'

'I am not good enough.'

'In that case, neither am I. Oh Harriet, we are neither of us perfect. I do not promise that I will never give you cause to be angry with me again, any more than I expect you not to be angry if you have a cause. It may even be that I could be angry with you, at times, with or without cause, for we are only human. But a moment of anger need not destroy our love, or our friendship. Indeed, I think it could make them stronger. Can we not make our dream into reality?'

For the first time she relaxed the stiffness of her attitude. Her hands were no longer behind her back, but clasped at her breast, and her lips trembled. He held out his hand again, and shyly she put her own into it. He pulled her gently towards him and smiled down into her face.

'What does it matter what the world calls us?' he asked softly. 'Sir Robert, Lady Harriet, they are just our outward labels. With each other, we are just Robert, and Harriet, friends and lovers. Is that not enough?'

She gave a little sob. 'Oh yes, Robert. Yes!'

He pulled her closer, and she did not resist. Clasping her firmly with one arm, he put his other hand under her chin to tilt her face up to his kiss. His lips touched hers, gently at first, then more fiercely as again he felt her respond at once to his touch. They clung together for a timeless moment, and when he raised his head to look once more into her eyes they were again shining as they had done on the night of the ball, and in the woods. Drunk with joy, he murmured, 'I shall write an ode to your eyebrows.'

'Shall you? How charming, when they are so horrid.'

He kissed each one at the point where it tapered, then her brow between them, and the tip of her nose for good measure.

'Horrid? Not at all. Perhaps a sonnet. And you must promise me . . .'

'Anything. Anything! What . . . ?'

He caressed the heavy mass of her hair that was, as ever, slipping from its chignon.

'That you will not use it for curl-papers.'

She melted into laughter, as he had known she would. 'Oh, Robert, was it not the drollest thing? Poor Harry, how very disillusioned he would be if he knew!'

'I fancy the disillusion has already set in. He is in no danger in that direction now. It was never very serious, you know, and it is not uncommon for a boy of his age to fall for a beautiful face with nothing much behind it. It is only as one gets older and more experienced that one learns to appreciate the importance of character, and intelligence. Some men never do learn to, of course.'

'I don't think I ever had enough beauty to make any man fall in love with me for my face, so I must be thankful you found my character to your liking,' she said demurely.

'Never say so! When with my own eyes I saw Lord Istead trying to take the greatest familiarities! Shameless girl!'

She giggled again.

'I am afraid that was the champagne, not my pretty face! I have never thanked you for getting rid of him. I was not frightened, of course, but it could have been so embarrassing. In fact, it was!'

'I am afraid I was a little harsh. I was jealous, you know.'

'Of Lord Istead? But he is only a silly boy!'

'I was mad enough for anything. But never let me hear you say you are not beautiful again. If you do I shall know you are fishing for compliments. All I can say is that to me you are the most beautiful girl I have ever seen.'

She was much moved, and thanked him in the most appropriate way she could, with kisses that he accepted with complacency.

'If you think I am beautiful enough for you, then I am sure I am satisfied.'

'I don't think I should mind if you were plain. It is the you-ness of you that I love, if you know what I mean. I think the most important thing is that we think alike, and laugh at the same things. When we are old, and our romance is no more than a precious memory, we will still be able to talk and laugh together, and enjoy each other's company. That is my idea of love and marriage.'

She was much struck. 'We shall talk of this, and say how silly I was! And how we will be able to tease poor Harry!'

'Not yet, though. He has had a bad fright, and while I think it will do him good, he needs time to recover.'

'Of course. You have not explained how you came to see him this morning. Did he come to you? I cannot think that he would.'

He drew her down to sit beside him, within the shelter of his arm, and punctuated his reply with kisses, a state of affairs that she found very satisfactory. 'It was quite by chance. His hansom cab collided in the street almost outside my door. I was just coming to pay my daily visit to you, and recognised him at once. He was not hurt, but a little shaken up, and the driver was trying to get some money out of him. I could not pass by and not help, and besides, I knew he should not have been in London at all. I took him home with me, and I fancy he was happy enough to tell me his story, once I was able to tell him that I knew something of it already.'

'Oh dear, was he much annoyed with me?'

'Only a little, and he soon forgot that.'

'You were very kind, and generous too.'

'Not at all. He is a good lad, and has learned his lesson, I trust. Not that he did anything so very wrong, he merely was a little unwise in his choice of goddess. He will know better another time.'

'How did you persuade him to go back?'

'With difficulty! He was all for coming over here hot-foot, but I managed to persuade him that he must return instantly to Oxford, before his absence was noticed. Then, of course, I was able to convince him that he was really doing me a favour.'

'How so?'

'Why, in letting me come to your rescue, of course! I told him I wanted to appear as your knight, and slay the dragon to win your favour. He seemed to think it was a good idea.'

She blushed, and faced him earnestly. 'I had already told Crowborough that I wanted to see you, before Annie and her father arrived,' she told him. 'You do not think I am doing this merely out of gratitude, do you?'

He could not resist teasing her. 'Well, I was not very sure... No, of course not, you darling, maddening girl. Your butler told me the minute I arrived. I was just funning. What made you change your mind, by the way?'

'I wish I could say that I came to my sense without any help,' she said sadly. 'I missed you dreadfully, and was so unhappy I did not dare to see you, for I knew if I did I could not go on caring about what you had done, or what I thought you had done. Then a friend of yours came to see me, and talked to me.'

He was surprised. 'Who was that? I didn't know anyone knew. Unless it was—was it Charles Dulverston, or his wife?'

'No, I did not know they were your friends. Is that why—why I saw you at their party?'

He grimaced.

'Yes, it was. I prevailed upon Mrs Dulverston to invite you, to give me another chance to speak to you.'

'And found me in poor Lord Istead's arms! You did not have much luck, did you?'

'I am not complaining. But do not think you can sidetrack me. Who was it came to see you?'

'I am afraid I may not tell you. He was afraid you would not like his interfering. He made me promise not to reveal his name.'

'He interfered to such good effect that I can hardly be vexed,' he said, kissing her again. 'Whatever did he say, I wonder?'

'He just . . . told me about you,' she said vaguely. 'Explained things, about how you felt and so on. He showed me that the you I knew, the Mr Roberts if you like, was the real you. I think I had known that all along, really.'

It was not hard for him to guess that the unknown visitor was Barton. He pondered for a while, and decided to say nothing about it. Perhaps his manservant had exceeded his duties, but if so it was out of love for his master, and it had certainly been effective. Their shared wartime experiences had made them as much friends as master and servant. Would he not have done the same for Barton, if the need arose? Of course he would. He decided that he would say nothing to him, either in thanks or blame, for either would embarrass the man horribly.

'I think it is time for us to make a fresh start,' he said. 'I shall not go down on my knees again, for it is too comfortable like this. Darling Harriet, will you be my wife?'

'Yes, Robert. With all my heart.' She sealed her promise with a kiss.

HARLEQUIN
American Romance®

November brings you ...

SENTIMENTAL
JOURNEY

BARBARA
BRETTON

Jitterbugging at the Stage Door Canteen, singing along with the Andrews Sisters, planting your Victory Garden—this was life on the home front during World War II.

Barbara Bretton captures all the glorious memories of America in the 1940's in SENTIMENTAL JOURNEY—a nostalgic Century of American Romance book and a Harlequin Award of Excellence title.

Available wherever Harlequin® books are sold.

Take 4 bestselling love stories FREE

Plus get a FREE surprise gift!

PASSPORT TO ROMANCE
SWEEPSTAKES RULES

1. **HOW TO ENTER:** To enter, you must be the age of majority and complete the official entry form, or print your name, address, telephone number and age on a plain piece of paper and mail to: Passport to Romance, P.O. Box 9056, Buffalo, NY 14269-9056. No mechanically reproduced entries accepted.

2. All entries must be received by the CONTEST CLOSING DATE, DECEMBER 31, 1990 TO BE ELIGIBLE.

3. **THE PRIZES:** There will be ten (10) Grand Prizes awarded, each consisting of a choice of a trip for two people from the following list:
   i) London, England (approximate retail value $5,050 U.S.)
   ii) England, Wales and Scotland (approximate retail value $6,400 U.S.)
   iii) Carribean Cruise (approximate retail value $7,300 U.S.)
   iv) Hawaii (approximate retail value $9,550 U.S.)
   v) Greek Island Cruise in the Mediterranean (approximate retail value $12,250 U.S.)
   vi) France (approximate retail value $7,300 U.S.)

4. Any winner may choose to receive any trip or a cash alternative prize of $5,000.00 U.S. in lieu of the trip.

5. **GENERAL RULES:** Odds of winning depend on number of entries received.

6. A random draw will be made by Nielsen Promotion Services, an independent judging organization, on January 29, 1991, in Buffalo, NY, at 11:30 a.m. from all eligible entries received on or before the Contest Closing Date.

7. Any Canadian entrants who are selected must correctly answer a time-limited, mathematical skill-testing question in order to win.

8. Full contest rules may be obtained by sending a stamped, self-addressed envelope to: "Passport to Romance Rules Request", P.O. Box 9998, Saint John, New Brunswick, Canada E2L 4N4.

9. Quebec residents may submit any litigation respecting the conduct and awarding of a prize in this contest to the Régie des loteries et courses du Québec.

10. Payment of taxes other than air and hotel taxes is the sole responsibility of the winner.

11. Void where prohibited by law.

COUPON BOOKLET OFFER TERMS

To receive your Free travel-savings coupon booklets, complete the mail-in Offer Certificate on the preceeding page, including the necessary number of proofs-of-purchase, and mail to: Passport to Romance, P.O. Box 9057, Buffalo, NY 14269-9057. The coupon booklets include savings on travel-related products such as car rentals, hotels, cruises, flowers and restaurants. Some restrictions apply. The offer is available in the United States and Canada. Requests must be postmarked by January 25, 1991. Only proofs-of-purchase from specially marked "Passport to Romance" Harlequin® or Silhouette® books will be accepted. The offer certificate must accompany your request and may not be reproduced in any manner. Offer void where prohibited or restricted by law. LIMIT FOUR COUPON BOOKLETS PER NAME, FAMILY, GROUP, ORGANIZATION OR ADDRESS Please allow up to 8 weeks after receipt of order for shipment. Enter quickly as quantities are limited. Unfulfilled mail-in offer requests will receive free Harlequin® or Silhouette® books (not previously available in retail stores), in quantities equal to the number of proofs-of-purchase required for Levels One to Four, as applicable.

OFFICIAL SWEEPSTAKES
ENTRY FORM

Complete and return this Entry Form immediately—the more Entry Forms you submit, the better your chances of winning!
- Entry Forms must be received by **December 31, 1990**
- A random draw will take place on **January 29, 1991**
- Trip must be taken by **December 31, 1991**

3-HRG-2-SW

YES, I want to win a PASSPORT TO ROMANCE vacation for two! I understand the prize includes round-trip air fare, accommodation and a daily spending allowance.

Name_____

Address_____

City_____ State_____ Zip_____

Telephone Number_____ Age_____

Return entries to: **PASSPORT TO ROMANCE**, P.O. Box 9056, Buffalo, NY 14269-9056

COUPON BOOKLET/OFFER CERTIFICATE

Item	LEVEL ONE Booklet 1	LEVEL TWO Booklet 1 & 2	LEVEL THREE Booklet 1, 2 & 3	LEVEL FOUR Booklet 1, 2, 3 & 4
Booklet 1 = $100+	$100+	$100+	$100+	$100+
Booklet 2 = $200+		$200+	$200+	$200+
Booklet 3 = $300+			$300+	$300+
Booklet 4 = $400+	____	____	____	$400+
Approximate Total Value of Savings	$100+	$300+	$600+	$1,000+
# of Proofs of Purchase Required	4	6	12	18
Check One	____	____	____	____

Name_____

Address_____

City_____ State_____ Zip_____

Return Offer Certificates to: **PASSPORT TO ROMANCE**, P.O. Box 9057, Buffalo, NY 14269-9057

Requests must be postmarked by **January 25, 1991**

--✂--------

ONE PROOF OF PURCHASE

3-HRG-2

To collect your free coupon booklet you must include the necessary number of proofs-of-purchase with a properly completed Offer Certificate

See previous page for details